ALPHA : IMPOSTURE

There are two sides to every story

Marc Jaytin

Independently published

Copyright © 2021 Marc Jaytin

All rights reserved

The characters and events portrayed in this book are fictitious. Any similarity to real persons, living or dead, is coincidental and not intended by the author.

No part of this book may be reproduced, or stored in a retrieval system, or transmitted in any form or by any means, electronic, mechanical, photocopying, recording, or otherwise, without express written permission of the publisher.

ISBN- 9798465113014

Cover design by: EternityBoxArt

Mother, Father, thank you both for all of your love, support and free beer. This one is for you x

DANIELLE BROOKE PALMORE

Every house is the same. The walls, doors, windows, and the roof. It the contents within that make every house unique. The furniture, the colour palettes, the people. Memories are created and captured as photographs, ready to show us how happy we once were. To remind us of where we've been and who we love.

Behind every door, people gather to share stories, build relationships, and make plans. Smiles cover grief as sadness is temporarily muted in exchange for a moment of mental relief. But for some, those moments are short lived.

"Hello Miss Palmore, it's Miss Baker from the school. I'm afraid we've had an incident."
"Is it Dani? Is she ok?"
"Yes, she is fine, but I will need you to come in to pick her up."

Grace looked up at the clock on the kitchen wall. 1:25pm.
"What now?" asked Grace.
"Yes, if that is possible."

Grace paused for a moment, *"Yes ok. I will be twenty minutes."*
"Thank you, I'll meet you at the school reception. Goodbye." With that the call ended.

This isn't the first time the school had called because Dani had been causing trouble, but this is the first time Grace has had to go and *collect* her.
"What have you done now?" Grace said to herself.

Leaving her freshly made cup of tea on the breakfast bar, Grace stood up and reached for the car keys. The family photo that stood on the shelf next to the keys, reflected a different version of the family. Grace and Jason sat smiling with the youngsters Danielle and Nicholas, positioned in front of their parents. The smiling didn't last long once Grace found out that Jason had been having an affair with the very woman that owned the photo studio. No wonder the session was so cheap. Grace kept quiet when she found out about where Jason had been going, and who had had been doing, until the day of his birthday. When Jason announced he was going out for the night with a few people from work, Grace knew that this was not the truth. He was seeing her...

❖ ❖ ❖

10:15pm. Jason thanked the taxi driver and stepped out of the car. As he got older, his birthdays became less important, but this birthday was special. Jason and his mistress had decided to come clean about their affair and he was going to leave Grace, and their two children.

As he walked toward the house, he spotted two men pouring petrol over a pile of something, but he couldn't work out what it was, or who the two men were. On closer inspection he realised that the pile of stuff, was his stuff. His clothes, books, Star Trek collectables and acoustic guitar were within this pile.

"What the fuck guy, this is my stuff." shouted Jason.
"Yep." replied the man with the petrol can.
Jason was stunned, *"Stop pouring petrol on my stuff."*
"Nope." was the blunt reply.
The second man spoke. *"You're Jason, right?"*
"Yeah. What of it. You know that's my stuff."
"We know. Your wife has asked us to help her with a little project and as part of the agreement, I get to do this."

Jason doubled over in pain after receiving a swift punch to the stomach.
"What was that for," he gasped.
The man grabbed Jason's hair and made him look up at the bedroom window.
"Grace. What..."
"How could you treat this beautiful woman he way you have been treating her?"
"What the fuck are you talking about." shouted

Jason.
"You, going out and fucking this other woman. Leaving this lady at home, alone. You should be ashamed, you dirty piece of rat shit."
"That's not true?"
"Bullshit, Romeo."

Jason received a second thud to the stomach.
"Now watch this you little bastard, and once you're done you can fuck off back to that bitch you've been shagging for the past few months."

Jason realised that he'd been caught and was paying for it in the worst possible way.
"My kids. What about my kids?" Jason yelled at the man holding the petrol can.
"Yep, they on the pile as well." he laughed.

With that, a lighter was dropped onto the sleeve of a white shirt. Jason was released from the physical restraint, and he ran toward the bonfire, screaming.

"Danielle! Nicholas!"
He paced frantically trying to work out what to do. Surely, he hadn't just witnessed the death of his own children.

"Grace, what the fuck. I'm sorry." Jason cried as he dropped to his knees.

From the upstairs window, Grace watched as everything Jason cared about was being destroyed.
"Mum, what is going on?"

Grace looked down at her daughter. *"Danielle, I told you to stay in with Nicholas and watch a film."*
"Yeah but..."
"No buts. Go and watch the film with Nicholas and in a minute, I will bring you both some ice cream. Does that sound good?"

Danielle didn't reply, she was staring out of the window. On the ground below she could see a huge fire and someone that looked like her dad shouting and screaming at the flames.
"What's going on Mum?"
"Step away from the window now and get to your room." Grace was getting impatient.
"Is that Dad?"
"It was." replied Grace, as the flames from the fire below gave the room a warm orange glow.

Outside, Jason made a run for the house but was grabbed by one of the violent strangers.
"Dani. Dani darling, it's me."
The young girl began to cry, *"What's happening to Daddy?"*

Grace had had enough. She closed the curtains and marched Danielle back to her bedroom.
"Now stay in there like I asked you to." Grace barked. She slammed the door to the bedroom, stomped downstairs and headed outside to confront Jason.

"Grace please. I didn't mean for it to go on this long."
With a firm hand, Grace slapped him across the face.

"I don't ever want to see you again. Stay away from my kids and stay away from this house."
Holding his cheek, Jason could only offer hollow apologies. The two strangers grabbed Jason and looked at Grace.

"Cuz, what do you want us to do with him?"
"Break his arms then take him back to that slut he's been with."
"Wait, no. What. Grace please, stop." begged Jason.

Grace turned away and walked back to the house. As she did, she heard Jason scream in agony. Not once, but twice. Taking a deep breath, she entered the house, looking back one more time to see Jason being driven away.

From upstairs, Danielle was also watching everything that had happened.
The fire, the violence, the screaming. Her Dad, Daddy, being beaten up. Having his bones broken then taken away, left her feeling numb. So much so that she didn't hear her Mum walk in behind her.
Grace stopped at the doorway and stared at her daughter.
"Danielle, I am so sorry you had to watch that. Darling? Please don't ignore Mummy....

This photo of the four of them is the only

reminder that Jason was ever in their life and acts as a visual warning about what would happen if she trusted men again. Jason left six years ago, and Grace has never allowed another man to enter her life.

Nicholas doesn't remember his father. He was only three when *that* happened. Danielle was older, aged eight. She remembers all of it.

"Hello, my name is Grace Palmore and I'm here to see Miss Baker."

The school receptionist looked through the names on a sheet of paper.

"Ah yes, if you could take a seat, she will be with you shortly."

Grace sat down and looked around the vibrant reception area. Photos and certificates of school achievements covered the bright yellow walls. A pile of brochures and the school magazine were placed on the table, begging to be read.

"Miss Palmore."

Grace stood up, *"What's happened?"*

"If you could come this way, Dani is in the headmaster's office."

This wasn't good. Grace had been called to the school a couple of times before, but it was never accompanied by this sense of panic. What had she done this time? Grace feared the worst.

"Miss Palmore, welcome. My name is Professor Mer-

rick, and I am the senior master at this school. It is not often that I get involved in matters concerning pupils as I have faith in my team to keep these issues from my door, but today is an exception."

Grace took a seat next to Dani who didn't even acknowledge that her own mother had entered the room.
Professor Merrick passed Grace a small, clear sealed bag containing a small amount of white powder.

"What's this? Danielle, what is this?" asked Grace.
"This," said Professor Merrick, *"is crushed white chalk."*

Grace was lost for words as Dani chuckled.
"Danielle here, has been targeting the more vulnerable pupils and threatening them."
"With this little bag?" Grace was confused.
"Yes Miss Palmore, but it is the way she has been doing it."
"Sorry but I still don't understand."

"Danielle has demanded the pupils give her what she wants, or she will plant this bag in their locker, thus resulting in a locker search that will no doubt get the child expelled from this school."
"But you know it isn't drugs so how…"
"Miss Palmore," Professor Merrick asserted his authority. *"Danielle has been manipulating the children to do her bidding. Most of these are youngsters from lower years and are easily intimidated by older*

pupils."

Grace shook her head, *"What do you mean, her bidding?"*

Professor Merrick explained. *"By using this method of intimidation and threat she has been able to acquire four smart phones, a set of wireless headphones and more than one hundred pounds in cash. We found these items in her locker along with more little bags. Some containing chalk as we have here, and others contain pills. The pills are nothing more than over the counter laxatives but the colour and shape of them is unusual enough that for a child who doesn't know better, they will believe whatever Danielle tells them they are. Danielle is refusing to tell us where these stolen items have come from and for how long this has been going on for."*

"How, how did you find out?" asked Grace.
"A pupil in Danielle's year alerted us to what she was up to."

Dani looked up, flicking her red fringe away from her eyes as she did so. *"Who was it?"*

Her question was ignored as Professor Merrick continued.

"After careful consideration we have decided to expel Danielle indefinitely from this school."

"Wait, what! You can't do this." Grace said in a panic.

"I can and I have. You will receive a letter in the post within the next few days explaining my decision and

what happens next. You will be advised to keep Danielle away from public areas for the next five days and the local council will discuss with you the next steps."

"What so that's it? Dani is not allowed to go to this school anymore. What am I supposed to do now?"
"Not my problem Miss Palmore. Miss Baker, if you could escort Danielle out of the building, thank you."
"But..."
"That is all Miss Palmore. Goodbye"

Once outside the school gates Grace looked at Dani. The once innocent little girl was lost and, in its place, stood this angry, obnoxious, teenage girl.
"What?" grunted Dani.
"Why have you done this to me?"
"To you? I didn't do anything to you."
Grace noticed the receptionist looking at her through the window. *"Come on let's get out of here."*

"I'm not going anywhere." replied Dani.
"Get your ass in the car, now!" Grace was done playing games.
"What if I don't? You gonna break my arms?"
Grace turned to face Dani. *"What did you say."*
"You heard."
"Listen to me," by this point mother and daughter were stood nose to nose, *"You get in this car now or I will force you if I have to."*

Dani didn't flinch.
"No. If you grab me, I will scream and that will look good in front of the school won't it. Social services will

get involved and they'd probably take Nicholas away from you."

"You horrible little bitch. Get in that car now or god help me I will drag you by the hair if I have to."

Dani smirked, *"Nicholas is a little pussy. He wouldn't last five minutes without his mummy."*

With that, Grace swung her right hand across the face of her teenage daughter.
Dani's eyes began to fill with tears.
"I hate you. I HATE YOU!" Dani screamed.
"What's going on?" Professor Merrick was marching out of the school gate.

This distracted Grace enough to allow Dani to grab her bag and run. She had no plan in mind but the more she ran, the further away she would be, and right now and that was all she wanted.

It's been suggested that she went to stay with her uncle, the same uncle that snapped the arms of her father all those years ago. There were also rumours that she was able to track down her father and stay with him. No one knows.

Grace sold the family home and moved with Nicholas to Kent. Dani never spoke to her mother again.

Many years of silence followed. The family unit was destroyed for good.
The funeral for Grace Eloise Palmore was a quiet affair. Her son Nicholas, a few friends, and distant members of the extended Palmore family were the

only people in attendance. There was no Jason, and no Dani.

MR DUDE RAY

Augustus Gordon Hayhurst never really liked his name, but on this particular morning, there were bigger things to worry about.

On his doormat lay 5 brightly coloured envelopes. One pink, two yellow and two baby blue. It wasn't his birthday, that was a couple of months back, and he wasn't celebrating anything; he lives alone with no spouse or dependants. Instead, today was the annual celebration of a certain **Mr Dude Ray**, an internet sensation. Well, maybe sensation is the wrong word to use but he was the creator of something we've all come to know now as Murder Day.

It started off with the first event taking place on November 18, 2006, in which, during a live stream **Mr Dude Ray** killed a spider. Doesn't sound like much but every kill must start somewhere.

In 2007 he went live and killed again. This time a wild, grey mouse. His method of killing wasn't anything creative or particularly enjoyable, he released the tiny critter from the humane trap, and stamped on it.

2008 was a budgie, followed in 2009 by a pigeon and in 2010 a kitten. The internet was made for cats and the moment he stamped on the head of that mewing tabby kitty, the world took notice.
For a whole year people speculated about what they had just watched and when the old video clips were found, **Mr Dude Ray** became something of an invisible celebrity.

Unfortunately, November 18, 2011, took too long to come around and by the time it did, **Mr Dude Ray** was pretty much forgotten. Undeterred, **Mr Dude Ray** (let's call him **MDR** from now) went ahead and killed a rabbit. Held it up by the ears, put a blade into its mouth and pushed down as hard as he could, tearing the mammal in two.

The following year a squirrel was sacrificed live and the following year, a dog. A young black Labrador Retriever that was so happy to play when **MDR** walked into the room, but soon realised something was wrong. As the tail of the animal dropped between her back legs, **MDR** sat beside the quivering bitch and force fed it a lit firework…

"I'm not reading anymore," Harper threw the book down onto the bed, *"why are you making me read this shit?"*
Dani walked out of the bathroom smiling, *"I said I'd make you famous and this is where it begins."*

"But this is just a piece of fiction written by a man fascinated with shock, gore and horror."
"Yep, but believe me, there's more to it than that."
Harper continued with her criticism of the book. *"You said you had something special to share with me, but this is bullshit."*

Dani positioned herself on the end of the bed.
"Listen, I want you to read this then we can chat, and I will tell you something that will change your world forever."
Harper was confused yet intrigued and curiosity was always going to win.
"Ok, so he basically kills this dog, then a pig, and follows that with murder."
Dani interrupts. *"That's where I want you to read the rest of this properly."*
Harper looked at Dani and with a slow, deliberate blink, her eyes move back down to the book in front of her. With a deep sigh and a shake of her head, she continued to read.

MDR finally got to that day when he killed his first human, and it was broadcast live for all to see. He recorded it all on camcorder and it wasn't a great viewing spectacle, it was very shaky, and the sound was horrible. It was filmed in a public toilet, so every time the knife was forced into the neck of the tramp, he would let out a tortured wail, and the sound would bounce around the ceramic shit house and into the very veins of **MDR**. He felt a surge of power, like the tramps very soul was being injected into him. This felt good. So good.

A lot of people got to see the video and was quickly labelled as being fake, I mean, who would do that and then post it online? Well, HE did.

The following year he did it again, and again the year after that.
Now he was internet famous and every year he did not disappoint.
Every death got more and more intense as the kills became more and more extreme and diverse. He killed with a hammer, he killed by throwing someone from a balcony. He even used cyanide on one occasion, but being the entertainer that he is, he saved the best for last.

In 2026, **MDR** went live with an estimated 66 million people watching. He was stood at the centre of a bridge, some 620m above the ground, staring into the camera. Now and then he would wobble which allowed the viewers to catch a glimpse of the concrete far below him.
He held the camera up to his face and shouted;
I have carried the souls of my victims and now the final soul to be consumed will be my own.
Embrace me as I fall into the Styx where I shall be carried home by the Ferryman. This is my return to Zion!

And with that he fell.

His body was recovered a few hours later where he was pronounced dead at the scene.

As a tribute to **Mr Dude Ray**, Murder Day was created and on this most special of days it became customary to send people vile, abusive, and threatening letters or cards.

Augustus Gordon Hayhurst (August to his friends) looked down at his doormat and wondered why this year he got 5 cards. He always got one from his mother, but the other 4 were a mystery.

One thing to remember with Murder Day cards is that these are designed to offend and create mental tension.

Fun side note: a company by the name of **RotAromA** produced a new line of Murder Cards that were not only keeping with the tradition of being offensive but also came in 6 different odour options.

1. **Uranus Egg**
2. **Corpse Lily**
3. **Festival Toilet**
4. **Warm Sewage**
5. **Anal Gland Discharge**
6. **Tramp Vomit**

Would you consider the sending and receiving of greetings card a hate crime? Well, the capital of this once great nation registers approximately 50 hate crimes on an average day, yet on Murder Day this number increases tenfold.

August is weak. The cards waiting and festering on his doormat scare him.
After a few minutes he realises that he can't spend the whole day just staring at the envelopes. Walking slowly over to the cards, he crouches down.
They stink. At a guess, anal gland discharge?
As August continues to squat over his Murder Day offerings, he hears something he didn't want to be hearing right now.

Knock, knock, knock.
August froze with fear. The door is knocked again, this time louder.
It's 8:43am, the day has only just begun.

"Is that it?" Harper is more agitated than she was a few minutes ago. *"It just ends with no conclusion. Please explain to me what it is I'm supposed to be getting from this."*

By this point Dani was dressed and applying the last of her black eye liner. "Harper, do you trust me?"
"No," Harper was quick to respond, "not yet."
Dani smirked, *"A classic case of lust before trust. Listen, I have to go so just chill today, read the book."*
"How long will you be?" asked Harper.
"I doubt I'll be back any time before 5."

Dani grabbed her bag from the bedroom floor and gave Harper and kiss on the forehead.
"Enjoy your day. Help yourself to food and drink. There's plenty in the kitchen."
Harper half smiled as she watched Dani close the door. *"I know there is,"* she said. *"It's my kitchen."*

Outside, the monotonous drone of London penetrated through the open window. Harper sat and considered her options for the day. Stay in and read this book or go outside and... and what? If truth be told, therein lies the problem. Harper was getting bored with London. As ridiculous as that may sound, this wasn't the life she wanted.
Born in Swindon, she lived in a spacious four-bedroom family home with her parents and older sister. The area in which she grew up was quiet, and not too far from the tranquillity of Wichelstowe Ponds. Many a summers night were spent sat at the water's edge, submerged in the moment, and enjoying the sounds of insects and birds float away into the clear blue sky.
Of course, London offers none of this. Yes, there are the Houses of Parliament, Buck House and countless museums. The Shard, Gherkin, and other silly looking buildings, but after a while they just blend and disappear into the grey background. There was no escape from the noise, hassle, and stress of living in London. A few times they had been able to slip away for a couple of days and head up the M1 to St. Albans, but those moments were

becoming very few and far between.

Harper closed her bedroom window, and stared at the book, *"Right, let's get this done."*

The Tale of Lola the Dog

Dale Stone was, and *was* is a very important word here, a respectable member of the community. Respectable in that he was a regular at the local church, had a part time job as a caretaker in the nearby school and still lived at home with his mother and sister. He was quiet, non-intrusive and always first to volunteer for any local events. He also killed small animals on a regular basis.

"Oh for fuck sake, here we go again," Harper mumbled to herself.

Dale Stone is a sick motherfucker and deserved everything he had coming to him. Sadly, it isn't much as the maximum jail term he will likely serve is five years. He is thirty-one now so still plenty of life left for him to enjoy once he has served his time.
It's true that he won't have a job to return to once he is released, and I can't imagine the church will be particularly welcoming once he returns, but

you never know. The church has been known to forgive worse.

Let us back track a little to sixteen months ago. No, that's no good. That's when he was arrested. Let's go back twenty-two months to when he killed a hamster.
An innocent, ginger haired hamster.

No, no. Let's go back further. Let's go back forty-one months from today. That's round about the time he had sex with his sister. Full penetrative, non-consensual sex that lasted almost two minutes. This wasn't the first time he'd had an illegal sexual encounter. Some years prior to this, he gave his virginity to a chocolate brown Labrador retriever called Lola.

Lola was the family pet and Dale Stone was very close to the animal. Very, very close. They would spend a lot of time together and one thing he learned was that if he poured meaty gravy over his genitals...

"Fucking hell," Harper shook her head, *"this is worse than the last one."*
She scanned the rest of the page hoping that if she did it quick enough, her brain wouldn't have time to digest what it was that it was being fed. All was going well until she paused after reading the word, *huppies.*
"Huppies. What are Huppies?" Curiosity got the bet-

ter of her and she continued reading.

... Lola got pregnant and after three months gave birth to five mutant huppies. Of those born, only one survived and it was quite unique. Its saggy skin was the colour of sewage diluted pink lemonade and it had patches of damp beige hair in the most random of places. It had two short stumpy arms but only one hand. The back legs were perfectly formed. By perfectly formed, what I mean is they looked like a couple of boomerangs inserted violently into the eye sockets of a dead bloated bullfrog.

Harper stopped reading, threw her head back and took a few deep breaths.
"This is not enjoyable... This is disgusting."

Flicking through the pages, she stopped briefly to read the titles of the subsequent stories.

Domino Cortez. She/Her. They/Them. Shot/Dead.

King of the Trolls

Frank Hunt. Baby Sniper

Herbie Rides, Again

Am I Dead?

"This is ridiculous." She looked across the room and focused on the photo of her and Dani on their first date night. *"What are you doing to me? Why do you*

want me to read this horrible stuff?"

Harper threw the book down and headed to the kitchen. A couple of minutes later she emerged holding a large glass of Oaked Chardonnay in one hand and the TV remote in the other. But what to watch?

ITV, BBC, Netflix, Amazon, Apple TV. Too much choice but not enough to enjoy. Harper finally decided on an old episode of Friends. After what felt like an eternity waiting for the adverts to end, the program begins.

The episode name; The One with the Truth about London.

"*Ha!*" Harper smirked at the TV, "*The truth about London. How ironic is that. Is there truth within London? Hurry up and get home Dani, I want the truth.*"

6:45pm. Harper is on her third large glass of Chardonnay and attempting to defeat The Chaser all on her own. As the programme reaches its finale the arm of the chair vibrates. It's the phone and a text from Dani.

SO SORRY HUN, BEEN DELAYED. I AM IN ROMFORD SO SHOULD BE BACK WITHIN THE HOUR XXX

Harper shook her head. She knew this would happen but for once hoped it wouldn't. Dani would often leave without explanation. Switching off the TV, Harper looked down at the book that had upset her so much earlier that day. "*Do I dare continue to read you?"*

8:46pm. Dani crouches down next to the chair.
"Sorry I'm so late babe, it's been a shitty day. Harper wake up."
"What time is it?"
"It's coming up to nine. How long you been asleep?"
Harper stretched her arms and opened her eyes.
"Where have you been?"
"Let's go to bed and I'll explain everything in the morning."
"No, no. I need to wake up. What's going on"

Dani stood up, *"Let me go and make a coffee and I'll explain everything in a minute."*
"No, you explain now. You left me with this stupid book with no explanation as to where you were going and you turn up nine, ten hours later and expect me to just accept it. No. I want to know what's been going on."

Dani sighed, *"I went to see my brother."*
Harper was confused, *"Brother? What brother. You never mentioned you had a brother, ever."*
Dani looked back, *"I'm going to put the kettle on. Do you want a coffee?"*
"No, I don't think I do. There's some wine left so I think I'll have some of that. Anyway, don't change the subject. Who is this brother? Dani, who are you talking about?"

There was no response.

Harper took a deep breath and shook her head.
"Dani, you're pissing me off. What is going on?"
Still nothing. Harper was about to open her mouth again when Dani walked in with the drinks.

"You ok babe? You seem agitated."
"Yeah I am. You went out this morning. Left me with this freaking book and then come home telling me you have a brother. Yesterday none of this existed and now it does."
"How many barrels should I order?"
"What!" Harper was confused.
"How many barrels should I order? They will be empty, but I can easily fill them with cucumbers if you want me to. My brother by the way, he has cancer."

At this point Harper stands up, *"What the actual fuck are you going on about?"*
"How was the book?"
"I haven't got the energy for this. You've been out all day meeting your dying brother, ordering barrels and now you want to know what I think about the book. The book is shit. Is that a good enough review!"

"How many legs does a crab have?"

Harper cups her head in her hands, *"What the hell are you on. Explain to me what is going on or where you scored your drugs from or have you spiked me. Tell me what is going on."*

Dani stands motionless, without emotion.

"Please, today has been shit and I don't need you coming home and doing this."
"Doing what?"
"Dani, seriously. If I've done something wrong, then I'm sorry, but you can't come home talking nonsense and expect me to understand."

Dani still stands. Stubborn. Unmoving.

"Fucking hell. Please! What are you doing?"

Dani breaks her silence. *"Have you noticed that you went from aggressive to apologetic without me saying a single word."*
Harper acknowledges what she has heard but doesn't entirely understand.

"When I came home you were asleep. I kissed you and asked you about your day. After that I told you about mine and you got angry."
"That's because you were talking shit."
"No, you were being selective with what you paid attention to, because you'd been asleep and when we started to talk, you got aggressive with me."
"Look I said I'm sorry, but I don't understand what you're trying to say."

Dani tried to smile, *"Sit down and I'll explain. This was my life for so long. Manipulation, accusation, and fear. Every day, never knowing what was coming next but forced to believe it was all my fault. No physical abuse, it was all mental."*
"What was?" asked Harper

"The life I had with my last partner. He allowed me to be physically free, but I never realised that I was being mentally controlled by him."
"Right, I still don't understand what this is all about."

Dani continued, *"I just wanted to give you a glimpse into the life I had before I met you. I gave you that book to read for a reason and everything that followed was done on purpose. I have spent my day in Trafalgar Square, chilling by the fountains and people watching. Everything I have said to you since I've been home has been a lie. I have no brother."*
"And the barrels?"
"No, I haven't ordered any barrels. I wanted you to feel off guard. Feel uncomfortable and confused."
"Why?"
"The life I had before you was drenched in darkness, and you became my light."

Harper laughed, *"Fuck off. Don't start trying to be poetic and romantic. It doesn't work like that."*
"I'm not I'm just trying to explain what things were like. What life is like when your mind is being battered continuously and you end up doubting the very thoughts you have."

"So, you don't have a brother, you haven't ordered any barrels and, I can't even remember the other stuff."
"It's not important anymore."
"It is," replied Harper, *"Understand me ok. You came in talking shit after I spent the day reading this book and now, you're bringing your past into this. Going on*

about how you were mentally abused or something. It's a lot to take in."

Dani nodded, *"Ok yes I understand. I think I made a mistake bringing this up in the first place, I don't know. Look, what's done is done. We can't pretend it didn't happen."*

Harper reached forward and held Dani's hand.
"What happened?"
Dani looked up, *"Did you read the book?"*
"Some of it why, is it important?"

Dani paused and silently nodded, *"Yeah it is. I know the author."*
"What does that even mean."
"I need you to read more and then we will talk."
"I can't read more. It's the work of a broken, fucking degenerate who... you know I don't even know what the hell is going on."
"This is hard for me as well. I've never shared this with anyone, and I'm scared that I've shown you too much."
"You haven't shown me anything."
"I have," Dani stood up and walked away, *"you just can't see it yet."*
"Where are you going?"

Dani stopped walking but didn't turn back.
"I'm going to sleep. Tomorrow I will tell you everything but for now, please read the book."
With that Dani walked into the bedroom leaving Harper alone and confused.

Harper looked at her now empty glass and silently decided that she will give this book one more try, but not before she has got herself another drink.

THE MAN ON THE BENCH

The train pulled in at Filton Abbey Wood station.

"Morning Todd," shouted the Station Master.
"Jeez! You made me jump old man." chuckled Todd
"Sorry boy, just checking you're awake. Off to work?"
"Sure am. Another day, another story to break."

With that Todd jumped up the step and onto the train. The train wasn't full, but Todd needed a table seat as he had a few bits to finish before he got to the office. It was a 25-minute journey to Newport which gave him plenty of time.

"Do you mind if I sit here?" asked Todd
The man sat opposite looked up, *"No, not at all."*

Sitting down, Todd smiled at his temporary table buddy.
"Busy?" said the man.
"Pardon." replied Todd
"Just asking if you're busy. You look like you're setting up your office on this small table."

"Is that a problem?"
"No, no. You working?"
"Yeah, afraid so."
"What do you do?"
"I'm a journalist."

Without hesitation the man replied in a way that Todd was not expecting,
"Ah, journalist. How do you spell that? Is it C, U, N... I forget the last of that."
"Sorry but what is that supposed to mean?" asked Todd.
"Who do you work for? One of the big nationals?"
"That's none of your business."
"Who?"

Todd was not one to draw attention to himself and certainly did not know how to handle such a confrontational situation.
"I'm freelance if you must know."
"So, you scurry inside other people's dustbins trying to find a vague piece of information that you can turn into a headline and sell to the highest bidder."
"No, it's nothing like that."

"Fuck off." replied the man. His eyes narrowing as he continued to bore a hole through Todd.
"What is your problem?" asked Todd, his hands beginning to tremble.
"You are my problem. You are vermin. No, sorry that's really rude of me. I love rats and squirrels. You wish you were vermin. You are scum. People like you don't

fucking care."

Todd was shocked, *"Erm, I'm sorry what?"*
"You're not sorry. The lives that people like you have ruined. Rooting through the social media posts of the deceased in an attempt to spice up the story. Ignoring the feelings of grieving families. Pissing kerosene onto bonfires hoping it will ignite and erupt into the flames of war. Forcing your political agenda by hiding the truth and being the best friend to whatever bandwagon rolls into town."

Todd began to gather his belongings.
"You are out of order."
"Shut up. You hunt with your cameras and kill with your words. You are scum."
Todd had heard enough and attempted to leave when the man grabbed his arm.

"People like you are why this country is such a fucking mess. Reporting nothing but lies to support hidden agendas and to appease certain minorities. You wouldn't know the truth if it raped you and bit your fucking tiny cock off. Now fuck off."

With that the man let go of Todd and sat back into his seat, glaring, as the young reporter grabbed his bag and walked at pace into coach C.
Finding an empty seat Todd was able to catch his breath. Glancing out of the window he focused on a small outhouse in the distance. As his rate heart slowed, the panic and fear dissolved but, in its

place, he could feel anger.

Todd rummaged through his bag and pulled out a well-worn, chewed up pencil.

Chomping on the wooden stress reliever usually worked but, on this occasion, it did nothing.

"Excuse me." Todd spotted the train guard, standing at the end of the coach. *"Excuse me, hello."*
"Yes sir, how can I help?"
"There is a guy in the coach behind this one that has just verbally and physically attacked me. I've moved into here because he frightened me. If you check the CCTV, you can see what happened. I was sat at the table seat opposite him."

The guard knew the cameras did not work on this train but told Todd he would sort it out.
"Can you describe the gentleman in question." asked the guard.
"Well, he is certainly no gentleman." replied Todd. *"He has short brown hair and is wearing a dark hoodie. Not clean shaven and he has a big bag next to him on the seat. Probably aged around twenty-five to thirty years old? The man that is, not the bag."*
Todd's attempt at humour missed the mark completely and all he could offer was an awkward, sideways smile.

The guard quietly nodded and walked into coach D. Todd hoped this would be enough and he wouldn't have to deal with that man again. Picking his pencil back up he popped it back in his mouth and began to daydream.

The train announcement broke his moment of tranquillity as he realised that this was his stop. He collected all his belongings and waited for the train to come to a halt.

"Shit, my phone."
Todd forcefully yet politely barged past the passengers stood behind him and got back to his seat where his phone was sat waiting for him. Todd let out a sigh of relief.
As he joined the back of the queue to get off the train, he spotted the guy that assaulted him earlier sitting on a bench. Todd pulled his phone out of his pocket and by slipping his finger over the phone screen, he activated the camera.

On leaving the train, he slowly walked toward the man.
Using a technique he had developed after a very confrontational interview with a local business owner turned sour, Todd was able to take a few photos of the man without raising suspicion, and even though he knew he'd got away with it, he couldn't help but verbally alert the man to what he had just done.

"I have your picture," Todd blurted out. The man raised his head and stared hard at Todd.
"I have your face. Fuck you."
The man on the bench didn't move and Todd walked away feeling he won that encounter. Next

stop, work.

Once at the office, Todd made his way straight to the staff kitchen and grabbed a bottle of cold water from the fridge. Charlie looked over at him.
"You ok Todd?" she asked.
"Yes. Oh sorry, good morning. Yes, I just had a run in with some guy on the train. No biggie"
"Have you got much on at the moment?" Charlie asked.
"Just the usual. Pants, shoes... a shirt. No sorry, nothing. Not nothing. What I mean is..." Todd had confused himself. *"Yeah, what I'm doing can easily be picked up by someone else."*

Charlie looked at her young reporter. *"You, sure you're ok?"*
"Yes, absolutely."
"Right, well, I think you need a change of direction so I'm pairing you up with Monica to work on the upcoming local elections. Take a break from covering sports as I know it's not really your thing."

Finally! All the stress from the confrontation on the train had now passed as Todd was elated to moving away from sports.
"It's not my thing, no, but I am happy to be on the team. Get it, team? Sports? Puns!"
Charlie grinned *"Yes, very good. Now go get yourself up to speed with what's going on and I'll catch up with*

yourself and Monica this afternoon."
"That's great Charlie, thank you so much. I'm really excited."
"I'm glad you're excited but take this seriously." Todd stood up straight and saluted, *"Yes boss."*

Three years ago, Charlie pieced together a rag-tag group of ambitious yet inexperienced writers, photographers, and journalists, and from nothing she has been able to establish the Newport Daily as a reputable newspaper. Early in life, Charlie made a few mistakes. Although she wouldn't consider her daughter one of these mistakes today, she and many others did when she fell pregnant at the age of 16. Her boyfriend walked away after Charlie refused to terminate the pregnancy, and she hasn't seen him since. Apparently, he moved to Scotland and that's all she knows.

Her daughter and her job are all she needs in her life right now. Her parents live locally, and she has a strong network of friends. She is the manager of her own journalist team who are loyal and respectful, what more could she want? That question isn't rhetorical, and if you were to ask Charlie what she truly wanted then that would be to break a story that had national interest, not just those who live in Newport. She wasn't ungrateful or unhappy. She just wanted more, but for now, this is the right place to be.

"Todd, did you know that Charlie has family in Gloucester."

Todd looked at his colleague and shrugged his shoulders.

Monica continued, *"Her cousin lives and works close to where that man was poisoned."*

"The alphabet victim guy?"

"Yes. Don't you think it strange that she hasn't shown any interest in chasing that story seeing as it is of National interest and in the interest of her family."

Todd pondered the question for a moment.

"No not really. We are a local paper and Gloucester isn't on our patch, so it would be weird posting news from another country."

"Would you consider Gloucester as being in a different country?" asked Monica.

"It's in England isn't it. This is a Welsh paper and as far as I know he hasn't ventured over the border."

Monica chuckled, *"But wouldn't you love to sink your teeth into a juicy story like that."*

"Hmmm, yes I would but I'll wait for the Welsh alphabet killer to make a start, then we can catch him."

Unawares that Charlie was listening in on the conversation, Monica made a fatal error.

"I just don't think Charlie has the ambition or motivation to chase the big story. She's got her kid, her flat and that'll do."

"That's a bit unfair," Todd replied. *"She has built all this from nothing, whilst having a kid at a really young age."*

Monica was unfazed and continued with her verbal

assault of Charlie.
"Kids are a convenient excuse. I'm just here until a vacancy opens at a proper paper then I'm off.
"Ok, I think I've heard enough," said Charlie as she walked into the office.
"Shit, sorry Charlie." Monica winced, knowing she had messed this right up.
"Monica if this role is too small for you then please feel free to move on. We have a commitment to our community, and you're right, it's not for everyone but I'm happy. Sorry if that doesn't fit in with your personal ambitions."

Monica was embarrassed, *"Look I'm sorry. I didn't mean for you to hear it."*
"Oh, and that makes it alright does it?" Monica attempted a response, but Charlie turned her attention to Todd.
"Will you be ok covering the election build up on your own?"
Todd looked at Monica then back at Charlie, *"Erm, yeah of course."*
"Thanks Todd." Charlie then left the office.

The room felt tense, and the tension finally broke when Monica punched the table.
Without saying a single word, she grabbed her bag, coat and stormed out of the office.

Todd sighed to himself, *"What a day."*
Looking across the room he saw Charlie coming back toward him. He offered a wry smile, but he

knew this wasn't going to be fun.

"Monica has left and will not be returning. You will be the head reporter on the local election stories. Well done, Todd, you just earned yourself a promotion."

"Wow, thank you Charlie. I would have preferred it to have been under different circumstances but, you know."

Charlie nodded in agreement, *"Listen, stay focused, stay honest and you'll do well in this job."*

"Thanks Charlie," replied Todd, *"I won't let you down."*

"I know, just make sure you don't let yourself down."

As Charlie closed the office door behind her, Todd was left alone to reflect on what had just happened. If truth be told, he never understood why Charlie showed little interest in chasing the Alphabet Killer story.

Is it because she is genuinely happy with her life right now, or is the story too big for this little paper?

Maybe she is waiting for that opportunity to work for one of the big boys?

Maybe she doesn't want to drag her family into this.

Todd smiled to himself, *"Maybe I should just get on with this, and stop thinking about that."*

Flipping open his laptop, he began his research.

I KNOW THE AUTHOR

It's 5:03am and Dani wakes to find Harper asleep in the bed next to her. Still dressed in her khaki velour loungewear, she looks so peaceful.
"I'm sorry that this is how things have turned out." Dani whispers, as she leans over and gently kisses Harper on the cheek. *"We will get this sorted, I promise."*

With a sigh, Dani pulls back the covers and heads to the kitchen.
First decision of the day, cup of coffee or tea? Dani filled the kettle and reached for a cup but stopped as there was a note stuck to the cupboard door.

> **Dani, I don't know what is going on but tell me today or I'm going back to Swindon and we are done.**

Dani frowned, grabbed a cup, and filled it with water from the tap.
As she stood sipping her drink, she read the note again.
Ignoring the freshly boiled kettle, Dani pulled the

note from the door and headed to the lounge. There sat the book, **Portrait of Them**. The book that, without any effort, had created an atmosphere of tension and stress. The book that Dani wished she had never seen but it's too late for that. There was a scrap of paper inserted in between the pages. She opened the book and began to read.

Frank Hunt : The Baby Sniper

During the winter of 1999, former army sniper Frank Hunt believed he was on a mission from God when he shot his first civilian. The victim survived but the baby she was carrying did not. Mary Macnamara was 33 weeks pregnant with her second child.
Twelve days later Frank struck again. Firing off 3 shots, killing 2 people and injuring another. Aisha Shafik was one of those shot and killed that day. She was 24 weeks pregnant.
Twenty days later Casey Blackman was gunned down. Shot multiple times and was 31 weeks pregnant.
Six days after, Lexi Hill was shot in the stomach. She survived but the baby she was carrying did not.
Three days later, he shot and killed Daisy Armstrong who was 27 weeks pregnant.
Nine days later, Franks body was dragged out of the Thames.

At the time there was nothing tying Frank to these shootings. The early conclusions were that Frank was just *another* white middle-aged man who couldn't face living any longer so decided to take his own life.

"Why do they have to make it so public?" asked DI Langstone.

"Make what so public?" asked Cream Tea.

"Suicide. It should be done in the privacy of your own home. Not out on display. Dragging other people into your dramatic sadness is the final act of a pathetic life that was no doubt full of bad decisions and ends with you standing on the edge of something, staring blankly into the distance as you mentally say goodbye to the world. A world, if truth be told, that doesn't give a monkeys bollock if you splat, bounce or walk away."

"A bit harsh isn't it boss?"

Langstone grinned at his junior *"Where's my coffee?"*

As Langstone sat waiting for his mid-morning refreshment he picked up the report on Frank Hunt. Without saying a word, Langstone got up and walked out of the office.

"Here's your coffee sir..." Cream Tea sighed and placed the cup next to the other cups that were full of unwanted coffee.

When Franks body was examined, he was

found to be wearing something highly unusual, and can only really be described as an artificial silicone pregnant belly bodysuit. Not the whole body, just the belly area. The rest of the body belonged to Frank. The 6-foot, hairy, heavy build, Frank. On the surface of the silicone belly there what appeared to be pen marks. A five-bar tally gate and two other separate lines, about an inch in length. Seven, it totalled seven. But seven what?

Fast forward 18 days and Frank was confirmed to be the person behind the murders of 4 people and seriously injuring 3 others.
The 7 tally marks scribbled onto his silicone belly, could they be the 7 lives he attempted to take?
Of those who survived, there was one male, and he was shot in the leg so Frank would have known that this wouldn't have killed him. Frank was a well-seasoned professional, so clearly took that shot on purpose.
The focus of Franks attacks were on pregnant women, but that only accounts for 3 fatalities.
Maybe he wasn't trying to kill the mothers, but the babies?
Foetal deaths from these attacks still only add up to 5, so were there 2 that haven't been found yet?
Databases searched, phone calls made and still nothing.

Franks last known address; a ground floor studio flat in Croydon revealed nothing. Literally nothing. When Police entered the property, it was

empty, apart from 3 items left of the laminate floor in the bathroom. A silver toaster, a broken Etch-a-sketch toy, and a framed photo of a heavily pregnant teenager. On the back of the photo were written these words.
> **'Half-sister. Bonded by blood, by envy.'**

Even to this day police have been unable to identify the young woman in the photo or been able to determine what happened to her.

Dani sighed, *"Why have I done this? Why did I made you read this?"*
"Is that an apology?"
Dani jumped. *"Sorry Harp, I didn't realise you were stood there."*
"Was that an apology?" Harper repeated.
"Yes, I think it was. I haven't read this for a long time and flicking through it again and reading this, I realise what I've exposed you to."
Harper sat down next to Dani, *"You ok?"*
Dani closed the book *"Yeah, I..."*

There was a pause, a deliberate pause?
"Harper look, I have had this book with me for a few years now and I've wanted to find someone who I could trust and share this with."
"Why me?"

Dani attempted to stand up, but Harper grabbed

her arm and pushed her back down, *"Why me?"*

"When we met at the club, I thought you were stunning, beautiful. I never had the intention of dragging you into this, but when you mentioned that you wanted to uncover a crazy story and create an online magazine on the back of that, I thought this would be perfect."

Harper responded quickly, *"Hang on a moment, don't pin this on me. I didn't ask to read this."*
"No, I'm not trying to... Listen, I want the best for you, and you wanted to create this magazine, so I added two plus two and... Well, I missed the point."

Harper was not impressed.
"I read this yesterday and I didn't like it. Murder, animal mutilation, incest, fucking hell there is even a chapter about filling someone with herbs or something. This is a horrible book. I don't even want to call it a book. Is it a book?"

Harper pulled her hand away from Dani and stood up.
"What the hell is going on Dani. What are you trying to achieve? As for the magazine thing, that was an idea I mentioned once. I have done nothing to make this a reality. It was nothing more than a passing fancy. A thought."
"I know the author."
Harper looked down at Dani, *"What?"*

"I know the author."

Harper had no response at first, but once she had digested the words that had just fallen out of Dani's mouth.
*"You do realise you told me that yesterday and I didn't care then. A friend of mine at college wrote a book called **The Nine Lives of Bobby the Blobby Fish**, but you don't see me force feeding you that crap, and believe me, it was crap."*
"This is different."
"Ok Dani. How is this different?"
"The authors name is Kane Azika, and he is a serial killer."

Harper tilted her head, *"I don't know what the hell you are talking about,"* she said in a calm and controlled manner, *"but you had better come up with some kind of explanation soon because you are really testing my patience."*

Dani looked down at the floor and took a deep breath.
"Kane Azika is the guy they call The Alphabet Killer."
Harper felt confused. She understands the words that were spoken but doesn't understand why Dani said them.
"What do you mean? I don't…"
"Let me explain best I can. I know, or should I say I knew him. We were together for a couple of years and in that time, I got to understand what he was about."

Harper interrupted *"What do you mean you were to-*

gether? Like friends or a couple?"
"Yes, we were an item, a couple."
"Is this who you were talking about yesterday? You shacked up with a serial killer? I knew you were bi but fucking hell Dani, do you have any standards?"

Before Dani could respond Harper continued her verbal assault.
"You know him. You know his name and you haven't come forward. You let innocent people die for some stupid reason. What the hell are you playing at Dani?"

Harper reached for her phone which prompted Dani to leap out of the chair.
"What are you doing?"
"I'm phoning the Police."
"Please don't." Dani held onto Harper's hand, *"Let me explain."*

Harper looked hard at Dani, *"Be straight with me or we are done."*
"That book I gave you, Portrait of Them, is the key to knowing everything you need to know about Kane. He wrote the book and believes that it's real."
"What? I don't understand what that means."
"Let me go and make us some coffee and I promise to tell you everything."

For a few minutes they both had some space to think as the drinks were being made. Harper picked up the photo from that night she met Dani at **MiiX**. A nightclub that prides itself on being *all inclusive and super exclusive.* It was a hot spot for the blossoming North London trans and alt community and was considered a safe space because, to put it in simple terms, the club was all about people being allowed to be themselves without fear of insults or violence. Sure, there were those who went out to cause trouble and, in some circles, **MiiX** was considered nothing more than a static freakshow, but those people were quickly found and removed from the venue. The fact that **MiiX** uses face recognition software, was well advertised and it was rumoured they had a team of people who would spend the night at the club and to the untrained eye, would look like regular club goers but these people were in fact wearing bodycams. Every night the footage was wiped, and no images were shared unless you were one of those who wanted to be disrespectful and cause trouble. If that was you, then you were kicked out of **MiiX** and your image shared across London and beyond. It was the perfect venue for what became the perfect relationship. In the photo they both look so happy. Isn't it funny how quickly things can change.

Dani handed Harper a hot cup of coffee. Very little milk with one large sugar.
"How about you tell me how you got involved with this. How did you meet this guy?"

Dani responded without words as her body language announced she was about to share something she didn't want to.

"We met one of those NHS clinics. The ones for people with mental issues."

Harper was taken aback. *"Were you a patient?"*

"No, I worked there. On reception. Every day would be the same thing. Mad person comes in, mumbles something about an appointment, finds a seat and waits. The whole time they are waiting they are either gently rocking themselves or staring at the floor. There were a couple of exceptions like this one guy who didn't smell good. It was a combination of body odour and cat food."

"Did he have a cat?"

Dani smiled, *"Ha, no. He lived on the 9th floor of a tower block but put a bowl of cat food out every day hoping that a cat would visit him, and for me that was the problem."* Dani sighed as she continued, *"I was a bit of a bitch at times because I didn't understand what they were doing. I found these people to be pathetic and most of the time they just needed to shut up, stop moping about and get a grip."*

"I don't think it's as easy as that."

"Harp, have you ever had the same guy, dressed in the same jeans, the same blue striped polo shirt and the same beige jacket come and stand by you talking about how lost hedgehogs follow him home. Has that happened to you?"

"Well, no." replied Harper.

Dani blew the steam from her cup and took a sip of coffee. She sat down, placing the cup on the floor next to the chair.

"It's the same story every week. Tuesday, 10:30am. His appointments weren't until 12 yet in he walked, bang on 10:30 and would share the same story. Did you know, after work he would wait at the traffic lights by the theatre for the hedgehogs, and when they were all together, he would push the button and wait for the green man to appear. When the green man started beeping, he would escort the animals across the road and back to their house. Apparently, all the hedgehogs lived together, and would all go out together, and could tell the time. People like that are a stain on the social landscape. Minds like children yet they're allowed to mix with the rest of us. They're a danger."

Harper didn't like what she was hearing.
"Hang on, I think you need to calm this down a bit. Why did you work there if everyone was such a... hang on, was he a patient?"
Dani nodded.

"I was so bored of the job. I'd been there for a year or so and it was the same routine, day after day. The same faces, the same excuses, the same office politics until one day he walked in and changed everything."
"Kane?"

"Yes. The first two visits he was polite, made interesting small talk and when in the waiting room, he always sat in the same seat. There were 22 seats in that waiting room, yet he would always go to the one on the left-hand side, 4 seats along."

The atmosphere in the room lifted as Dani sat back and took a deep breath.

"On his third visit he began chatting with this woman who was another patient. She was super quiet and nervous. Not sure why but Kane immediately warmed to her. I don't know if he could see her anxiety so tried to put her at ease or if he just fancied her? She was attractive enough I suppose if you like chubby bimbo looking blondes. Fat ass and no class. Not my type, but each to their own."

Dani paused to take another sip of coffee. She looked up at Harper who was shaking her head.
"What?"
"The way you talk about people. It's disgusting."
"Harp look, I'm trying my best here ok. You asked, I'm telling you. I didn't hate those people it was the situation I hated."

"Tell me more about Kane."
"After a few weeks of this the two of them seemed to be getting on really well and I could see more and more of his personality coming through. He was starting to become a bit of a curiosity. I would look forward to him coming in but on one of the weeks he didn't turn up for an appointment. The blonde was there and looked

lost without Kane. She asked me if he had an appointment today, to which I could not respond, patient confidentiality and all that, but it was the following week that was the strangest. He came in late for his appointment and was quite aggressive. Blunt and not particularly chatty with anyone. He didn't even talk to the blonde, just handed her a scrap of paper, and walked through the doors to one of the consultation rooms. Five minutes later I went for a break and as I was stood outside Kane walked straight past me and for some stupid reason I called after him."

Harper questioned her decision, "Why?"
Dani shook her head, *"I don't know. The words fell out of my mouth before my brain had a chance to stop them. Kane turned around and told me that he wouldn't be back, and that the system is a bag of dog shit, or something along those lines? I asked him if he was ok. He didn't reply and walked away. That's where I should have left it, but I didn't. I went back in, pulled up his details and copied down his phone number and email."*

"What the fuck Dani. Why would you do that. He was a patient in a mental hospital."
"It wasn't a mental hospital."
"Clinic then, whatever. The point is you should never have done that."
"Well, it's a bit late now isn't it. What's done is done and I'm telling you all this now so we can fix it."
"Fix it! He has killed people."
"I know. ***I fucking know!****"*

By this point Dani was becoming hostile. She picked up her coffee and looked at it with disdain.
"I need a stronger drink.," she muttered and walked off to the kitchen.
"A little early isn't it?" Harper could see that Dani was not going to listen so left her alone.

"Don't judge me Harper. He was what I needed at that time in my life. I had nothing and he offered me something. Something dangerous, unpredictable and new."
Dani swallowed a mouthful of vodka and poured some more into a tall glass. She turned to face Harper.
"I hate him."

"I want to know what happened for you to feel like this. One minute you're saying he was this great new addition to your life and the next you hate him. What happened in between?"
"Let me tell you one of the many stupid fucking stories I could tell you about him."
"Will I need a drink?"
Through teary eyes Dani chuckled, *"Yeah, you might as well. I'll get you one."*
"Please be honest with me," pleaded Harper.
"I've got no reason to lie," replied Dani *"When it came to Kane, fact was always stranger than fiction."*

Dani took a large gulp from her glass and began.

"Kane always used the dark web. He used stuff like

Bitcoin and had a couple of bank accounts that he wouldn't allow me to have access to. He would happily leave bank statements around so I would spot them but that was for his High Street banking, not the weird shit he opened online. I went round to his flat when he lived in Southampton and sat on the coffee table was a stack of cash. £1000 to be exact. Next to that he had a bit of paper headed <u>'things I could buy for 1k'</u> and on this list was a gun."

Harper was concerned, *"He didn't buy it did he?"*
"Yep. Well, he had already got it. He just wanted to show me what £1000 in cash looked like."
"But surely you know that?"
"Well of course but I think this was his way of waving his dick about showing me how wealthy he was."

Harper put her drink on the floor.
"I don't want to drink this. I need to be thinking clearly and get a grasp of what you're telling me. He has piles of cash just hanging around his flat and a gun?"
Dani nodded, *"A Glock. It set him back £850, which included bullets."*
"What did he do with it?" asked Harper.

Dani took another large mouthful of vodka. Coughed, then continued.
"He hid it in a pub toilet."
"What? What do you mean hid it in a toilet?"
"We went for a drink one evening in a pub on the High Street and after a couple of beers, he wandered off to

use the facilities. When he came back, he picked up my drink and swallowed what was left and whispered to me that we had to go, but to look normal. So, we left and went to a pub across the road from the pub we were just in. Kane told me to grab a seat near a window as he got us our drinks. Once he sat down, I demanded to know what was going on."

Harper interrupted, *"What did he say?"*
"Nothing. He winked and then pointed out of the window and as he did a couple of police cars pulled up along with a van. I asked him what was going on and all he did was smile and start drinking. Eventually he told me what he'd done which was hide the loaded gun in the pub toilet."
"Why?"
Dani shook her head *"Apparently to amuse himself and to give all the people something exciting to talk about."*

Harper stood up, *"Fucking hell, Dani. Who places a loaded gun in a public place and just chances that everything will work out. No one gets shot so that's ok. It gave everyone something exciting to talk about? Do you have any idea how stupid this sounds!"*
Dani nodded, *"I do, but it became the norm. Stupid shit like this is what he did. He got bored and also thought he was offering something to people by brightening their day."*
"By leaving a gun in the fucking toilet!" shouted Harper.
"Yeah. Look I'm not defending him, I'm just telling

you what happened. Telling you what things were like. For him this was nothing more than a game. He looked upon people as something lower than him. Something he didn't need to be concerned about. I was the only person he cared about, and I was the only person he had."

Dani fell quiet as she appeared to realise the horrible truth.
"I was the only person he had in his life. I was his."

Harper looked at Dani and saw, for the very first time that her bullish confidence had been replaced by vulnerability.
"What did he do to you. Dani, look at me. What did he do to you?" Harper asked quietly.
"I am so sorry. I never wanted to bring this much shit your way, but I needed to tell someone. I needed to share what I knew and get it sorted and you are the only person I trust."
"And," replied Harper, *"the only person you knew who was looking to launch an online webzine…"*

Dani stood up.
"No this Is not about that. At first yes, I needed an excuse to bring this to your attention, but I need help. Do you know how hard it is to carry the burden of murder? Murder you haven't even been a part of yet feel like you could have prevented."
Harper laughed, *"Could have prevented! Are you for real! Of course you could have prevented this. How many of these murders do you know have happened?"*

There was no reply. Harper grabbed Dani by the arm.

"How many of these do you know about?"

"I don't know. One, eleven... I don't know."

"Eleven!" by this point Harper was screaming. *"What the actual fuck do you mean eleven."*

"Look I don't know ok. I don't fucking know! This book, this stupid fucking book is all I have to go on and when I started seeing the news reports I started to piece bits of the jigsaw together and once they mentioned the alphabet thing, I knew who they were on about."

"How?" Harper spoke through gritted teeth. This was starting to feel like the beginning of the end for her relationship with Dani.

"There are a couple of chapters in this book that play with the alphabet idea. The main one being the one about GoD following the alphabet killings or something? Did you read that one?"

"No, I didn't" replied Harper.

"It's probably the closest thing to what he is doing right now. Ticking these places off the list. The game started in Andover, moved to Basingstoke, then Cambridge."

Harper interrupted, *"I know the route he took. It's been all over the news for the past few days."*

"Here," Dani passed Harper the book. *"Read it."*

Harper looked at Dani, then at the book. Taking it from her, Harper sat down and began to read.

"Who the fuck is Zachary?"
"Just read it and tell me it doesn't match what is going on right now."

Harper sat down and began to read. Dani took this moment to open the window and let in some fresh air which felt good, blowing across her face, cooling her down.

"I guess Zachary is the letter Z then. Is that what this means?"

Dani turned to face Harper who had finished reading, *"Yeah I think it does."*

"I see you got a mention in the little poem. Dani Duck was his first love."

Dani didn't know how to respond. *"If that's what it says."*

"What does that mean?" Harper frowned.

"You know what," replied Dani, *"I don't know, but can't you see. At the end of the poem, he lists the places he would go and visit to kill people."*

"Not really. These are different places." said Harper.

"Yes, no. No, some of them are different."

Dani grabbed the book from Harper.

"Look here, Cambridge and Exeter. We know they are places he has been. Please believe me Harp. I need your help."

Harper walked away and took a few deep breaths.

"We need to go and see someone."

"Not the police. I'm not going to the police."

"No, not the police," replied Harper, *"We're going to pay a visit to my dad."*

"What? Who's your dad?"
"Go and pack some things and I'll explain on the way."

Dani did what Harper requested. If she truly wanted help, then she was going to have to trust what Harper was saying. Let her make the phone call and see what comes of it.

"I've spoken with my dad, and he is happy for us to travel over to him tomorrow."
"Where does he live?" asked Dani.
"Swindon."
"Swindon! I thought he was local."
"It's not that far," replied Harper. *"What I suggest right now is we get some food and calmly go back to this once we've eaten.*
"Did you want me to go out and get something?" asked Dani.
"No. Let me go on my own. I need some space."

Without saying another word, Harper walked out of the flat. Dani looked out of the window and could see Harper crossing the street and heading towards the supermarket.

"What the fuck!" Dani screamed.
"What the fuck is going on? What am I doing?"
She picked the book up and threw it across the room. *"Fuck off Kane, FUCK OFF!"*
Dani collapsed to the floor as the emotion of the past few hours got the better of her and she began to cry. Her mind was blank and all she could feel was invisible pain. Never had she felt so betrayed,

not by Harper, but by herself. *"Why didn't I just throw the book away when I left him? Why did I have to do this?"*
Dani closed her eyes and wished for death.

"What the... Dani," screamed Harper as she saw Dani lying motionless on the floor. *"What's wrong, are you alive."*
Dani opened her eyes, *"Yeah, I'm still here. The stress became a bit too much, so I had a little sleep."*
"On the kitchen floor?"
Dani smiled, *"What food did you get?"*
"Hula hoops," replied Harper.
Dani laughed, holding back the tears she looked at Harper, *"I love you."*

For the briefest moment Harper looked away and then back at Dani, *"I got you some fizzy water as well to help sober you up a bit."*
Harper picked up the carrier bags she left at the front door leaving Dani on the floor.
"What did you get us for lunch?" Dani said as she made her way back to her feet, wiping her eyes with the sleeve of her top.
"I told you, hula hoops."
"Just hula hoops?"
Harper chuckled, *"Yep, but it's a big bag."*

As Dani entered the kitchen, she spotted the hula hoops next to a couple of packet sandwiches and a big bar of chocolate.
"They didn't have your favourite, so I got you a

chicken and bacon sandwich instead, is that ok?"
Dani quietly nodded, *"Yeah, perfect. Listen Harper I'm really sorry."*

Harper cut her off. *"Look, this morning happened. Things were said that cannot be unsaid, and we know that there is a lot more that is still left to say. So, can we just chill for half hour, watch some TV, eat some food then get back to this Kane stuff."*
"We don't have to."
"Dani listen. Tomorrow we are going to visit my dad and I want us to have a pretty good reason for dragging this all up for him to investigate."
Dani became concerned, *"Investigate. What do you mean investigate.?"*

Harper took a deep breath as she knew this would not go down too well,
"He's a retired Private Investigator. He used to work on a lot of very high-profile cases and dealt with surveillance, intelligence, and the logistical side of personal security. I don't really know what most of that means, but it paid well which is how he was able to retire so early. My dad will know people who he could speak to about this and see if your story holds up before we go to the police."
There was no response so Harper continued, *"He will be on our side as long as we go there with a solid story and some proof. He doesn't suffer fools gladly and will call you out if he catches a wiff of bullshit."*

Dani grabbed her food, walked into the lounge and

switched on the TV.

"Let's chill for half hour yeah?" Dani said bluntly.

Harper knew this was going to be a rough day but if they were to get through this then Dani would have to cooperate.

SWINDON

ACT I

The drive from London to Swindon is simple enough, it's getting out of London that takes the time. Harper hadn't planned on it taking more than ninety minutes just to reach Slough, but it did give her some time to get more information out of Dani.

"Tell me more about Kane. What happened after you hooked up?"
Without thinking Dani responded, *"We did what every new couple does, we had fun and shagged the whole time."*
Dani noticed Harper's grip on the steering wheel had tightened.

"Sorry. What I mean is, we were good for a few months, but then his behaviour became unpredictable and dangerous. I know he started a new job, but he wouldn't share the details."
"Didn't you find that weird?" asked Harper.
"At first yes, but over time I got used to it. That's what

Kane did. If he wanted you to know something, he'd tell you. If he didn't, then he wouldn't."

Dani continued knowing full well that the information was not going to be well received.
"I knew he had a couple of places in Southampton that he owned but I never got to go to the place he had near his job. It was only when I noticed he'd been cutting that I became concerned."
"What do you mean, cutting? Like self-harm cutting?"

Dani nodded, *"He'd done it before we met, and they looked like nothing more than a few scratches. The sort of thing you'd blame your cat for doing, but these, these were new cuts. Shorter in length than the old ones but a lot deeper, and more of them."*
"On his arms?"
"The old ones were but he was clearly moving beyond that. He carved an inverted cross into his chest once and the word ART into his calf muscle."

Harper didn't believe what she was hearing.
"What the actual fucking fuck Dani. Like, seriously. What else? What else did he do?"
Dani looked down and shook her head.
"This is what we are gonna do. There's a service station 2 miles ahead. When we get there, we will park up and carry this on. Until then, just say nothing."

Although only a couple of miles away, the journey itself felt so long and awkward. No one spoke and even after they found a parking space there was still no conversation.

"Shall I go and get us some drinks?" asked Dani.
"No." Harper was quick to respond, *"tell me again about this cutting. Did he ever cut you?"*
"He never cut me but for him, well, he got addicted and he enjoyed cutting. It was no longer a release or a way to deal with emotional stress, it became nothing more than a thrill I suppose? He enjoyed watching the blood pour from his arm, leg, chest or wherever and every time he did it, it just got more and more bizarre."

Dani knew what question was next...
"Like what?" asked Harper.
"One night he invited me round to his place and we watched a film, had a few drinks..."
Harper interrupted, *"Get to the point."*
"Ok," replied Dani with an evident sarcastic tone to her voice, *"We fucked, and then he cut across his stomach at the same time he ejaculated."*

Harper smacked the top of the steering wheel with her open hand, *"Fucking hell, do you not understand how fucking stupid this sounds. What are you talking about?"*
"He hid a razor blade under the pillow and had me in the standard missionary position with my legs up, feet next to his face. He liked that because he would talk to them during sex."
"Talked to who?"
"The feet, my feet."

Harper rolled down the window as she was beginning to feel very warm.

Dani continued, *"When he leaned forward, I couldn't see much and that's when he grabbed the blade. I didn't know anything about it until after when I heard giggling coming from the bathroom. When I went to see what was going on, he had drawn a smiley face on his stomach using the open cut for a mouth and with his blood, painted some eyes on his chest."*

Dani paused hoping Harper would inject something into the conversation, but she sat there, staring straight ahead, hands firmly clasped on the steering wheel.

"When he explained to me what he'd done, I got frightened. All that time he had a blade under the pillow, and I didn't know. He could have done anything with that."

"Did it hurt?"

"Did what hurt?"

Harper repeated herself, *"Did it hurt, when he cut himself?"*

"Um no, apparently not. He said it hurt after but at the point of climax there…"

"Yeah ok, you know what, I've heard enough." Harper relaxed her hands from the steering wheel and looked over at the Dani.

"Do you not get how absurd this all sounds?

Harper pleaded, hoping to get Dani to see things

from her point of view.
Dani shrugged her shoulders and gently shook her head.

"Do me a favour alright. Make sure all the info you have is correct. Check the places he killed, what weapon he used, who was the victim. That kind of thing."
"I've already done that," replied Dani.
"Do it again. Basically, don't talk to me until we get to my dad's and hopefully, he won't pick up on this tension between us. I don't want the first time you meet each other to be on negative terms."
Dani nodded, *"Ok Harp. No problem."*

Within a couple of minutes, they were back on the road and Dani was reading through the rough notes she had made.

Andover. Hammer. Male.
Basingstoke. Stabbing. Male.
Cambridge. Stabbing. Female.
Doncaster. Assault / Fell. Female.
Exeter. Burnt/stabbing. Male.
Folkstone. Hammer. Male.
Gloucester. Cyanide. Male.

There was no clear or obvious pattern to the kills, but one theory Dani made a note of was the pattern of three.
Male/Male/Female. Female/Male/Male.
If this was to hold true then;
H would be male,

I would be female.
Followed by **J** – female and **K**, **L** both being male.

Even if this did play out to be true it doesn't help prevent any future kills. Dani knew she was just clutching at straws. Maybe Kane did outsmart everyone on this? I mean you can't go and alert the entire female population of **J**...

It was then that Dani realised something. **J** – where in England begins with **J**? A quick online search suggested that the only towns that began with **J** were Jarrow and Jersey. There were a handful of villages listed but Kane hadn't visited a village up to this point so it was a safe assumption to make that a village wouldn't be on his hitlist.
"I know where Kane is going." Harper ignored her.
"Harper, listen I know where Kane is going."
"Dani, we are nearly here. Can we pick this up later?"

Dani went back to her notes as a smile crept across her face. *"I've got you, you bastard,"* she muttered to herself. Jarrow, it's got to be Jarrow. He won't be able to get in and out of Jersey without leaving a trail, so Jarrow is the only practical option.

Another stop created the perfect opportunity for the briefest of conversations.

"To clarify, so you don't forget, my dad was a top rung private investigator up until a few years ago when he decided to retire. He knows a lot of people who know a lot of people, and any one of these could help you

track down and capture Kane. If you truly believe it is him then I think this is how we get this sorted."
"Why are you telling me this? I know." asked Dani.
"No point reminding you once we've arrived is there."

Not understanding the point Harper was trying to make, Dani turned away and looked out of the window. Swindon looked like every other place. Houses, grass, walls, people. Nothing new yet she had never felt so anxious, but there was no point dwelling on it. They had arrived.

"Now remember," said Harper *"relax, we are all good. Things are great, let's be positive and once we're all settled, then we will get onto the weird Kane stuff."*

"Harp, I was trying to tell you that I know where Kane is going to be. Jarrow, he will be in Jarrow,"
Harper took a deep sigh and looked at Dani, *"Jarrow, when?"*
This was the part Dani hadn't worked out yet. "Ah, I erm…"
"Exactly." replied Harper as they walked toward the front door.
They both looked at each other and forced a smile. Harper knocked on the old wooden door.
"Don't you have a key?" asked Dani.
"No, my dad doesn't do trust."

There was no response so Harper knocked again. This time the door was opened. A well-groomed man dressed in dark jeans and a grey shirt stood in the doorway. Dani could see the *Neith* family resemblance, but he looked so tired. His blue eyes had lost whatever sparkle they once had, and he knew it. Maybe this is what happens when you have nothing in your life anymore? The light inside you fizzes away to nothing.

"Harper, it's so good to see you."

Harper introduced Dani to her father.
"Dad this is Dani, and Dani this is my dad, Keith."
"Keith Neith?"
The older gentleman shook his head playfully, *"No, she's been using that one since she was at school. My name is Richard."*
"Or Dickie." Harper laughed.
"Yes, that has been used before."
Richard stepped aside and welcomed the girls into his home, *"Come in, come in."*

The door opened directly into a large living room with dark wood furniture and cream soft furnishings. Nothing spectacular caught the eye, it was just a nice house.

"You have a beautiful home Mr. Neith." said Dani as she ran her fingers across the top of a nearby chest of draws. Looking down she realised that the wood was darker than it first appeared, the true colour was being hidden by the dust. Wiping her finger against her leg she looked up and smiled.

"I was just saying, this is a lovely big house you have."
"It's the family home," said Harper.

"It was the family home." Richard corrected his daughter. *"The house is a bit big for me now that everyone has left."*

Harper offered an awkward smile and moved toward her estranged father, hoping for a hug. It had been so long since they had seen each other face to face.

"You've travelled from London, haven't you? I'll go and put the kettle on."

Harper was left stood with her arms out but had no one to embrace.

"This is going to be a tough couple of days."

"Couple of days. What do you mean, a couple of days." Dani thought it would be a quick visit, not a sleepover. *"We're staying here? Does he know that?"*

"Course he does. Unlike you, I do plan ahead."

Richard walked back into the room holding a tray with all the necessary crockery needed for a tea party.

"Cute," muttered Dani.

Richard sat down and gestured that Harper and Dani do the same. Placing the tray in the centre of the coffee table, he sat back and stared at the two guests.

"Does the tea pour itself or something?" chuckled Dani.

"What do you want Harper?" asked Richard, totally ignoring what Dani had said. *"You need my help*

tracking someone down? You know I'm not in that game anymore."

Harper nodded. *"I know that dad. It's just that, something has come up and I need you to see if there is any truth in what Dani is saying."*

Richard raised his hand, *"Hang on, I'll stop you there. Start from the beginning and maybe then you will make more sense. Dani, can you pour the tea please."*

Dani raised her eyebrows and before she could say anything Harper whispered to her, *"Please, I don't want any arguments"*

ACT II

Forty minutes had passed since Dani poured the first cup of tea and now, she was in the kitchen making another. A watched kettle never boils, apparently. Dani watched the kettle hoping the old proverb would hold true, but sadly it did boil so she had to return to the living room and face Richard.

There was an evident clash of personalities, plus Harper had revealed that her girlfriend used to date a serial killer. An active serial killer.

"What are you doing?" said Dani as she walked into the room.

"I'm showing dad the book that you said was written by Kane." Harper replied.

Dani put the cups down on the table. *"Don't go through my stuff."*

Harper didn't appreciate the tone of Dani's voice. *"Yeah alright. This is important, isn't it?"*

Dani picked her cup back up and returned to the kitchen.

"Let me go and see what the problem is." smiled Harper as she stood up. Richard didn't respond.

"What's wrong?" asked Harper as she confronted Dani.

"Nothing."

"Well, that's a lie."
"Why did you give him the book. I was going to let him have it once I was comfortable knowing he would do the right thing. All I've done is sit there watch you two talk, as I fart about like a housemaid making tea."
"Tell me five things about Kane." Richard bellowed from his chair.

Dani looked at Harper. *"What the fuck?"*
"Can you come in here and tell me five things about Kane."

Dani did not appreciate being spoken to in that way.
"Sorry but do you actually have any manners?" she asked Richard.
"I beg your pardon," replied Richard.

Dani paused for a brief second before answering. As much as she wanted to have a row, she knew it wouldn't be the right move and this was all about what was best for her and Harper.
"What did you say you wanted to know Richard?" asked Dani through gritted teeth.

"Tell me five things about Kane."
"He wipes his bum standing up. Like, he stands at the opposite side of the room facing the toilet..."
"No," Richard interrupted. *"I want five things that would help us identify him. Age, height, build, places he likes to eat, drink. You know. Useful stuff, not where in a room he wipes his arse."*
"Ok, I'd say he's about six foot."

"You'd say he's about six foot or he is six foot?"

Dani raises her hand a few inches above her head.
"He's about this much taller than me. I'm five six"
"So, he isn't quite six foot then is he."

Dani looked over at Harper who gently shook her head.
"Anything else?" asked Richard.
"Yeah, he has short dark hair, naturally dark brown eyes but he owns and uses a lot of contact lenses so changes his eye colour often."
"Why?"
"Paranoia." Dani replied. *"Eye tracking technology and all that conspiracy rubbish."*
"You don't agree with that?"
"No."
"Well, it's true. It's all true."
Dani frowned, *"What do you mean?"*
"What else can you tell me about Kane?"
"I don't know. He's just a bloke. Looks like a bloke, walks like a bloke. He's in pretty good shape, toned. I don't know what else to tell you."

Richard reached over and picked up his pad of paper and a pen. Without saying a word, scribbled something onto the top page. Looking straight at Dani, he showed her what he had written.

NOTHING.

Dani stared at the page and shrugged her shoulders.

"Nothing. You have told me nothing." Richard said as he stood up from his chair.
"Dad, please calm down."
Richard continued to stare down at Dani, *"Tell me something I can use."*
"Like what?" Dani was starting to get agitated, and Harper knew it was just a matter of time before she said or did something she would later regret.
"Dani please," Harper positioned herself between them in an attempt to calm the situation.
Richard stands firm and says in a softer tone, *"Tell me what I need to know or get out of my house."*

Dani relaxes her shoulders and sits back down.
"Be specific. Ask me a question and I'll do my best to answer it."

Harper gently nudges Richard back towards his chair and whispers, *"Sit, please."*
Richard does as he's told and once again locks eyes with Dani. *"Where does he live?"*
"Southampton."
"Where?"
"He has a few addresses, but I only knew of the one in Ocean Village."
"And.."
"It's a penthouse. Valued around a million."
"How can he afford that?"
"His dad played a big part in the redevelopment of some areas in London. Chelsea, Knightsbridge, I think. Either way he has money from him."

Richard picked up his pad and began to write. *"Where is he now?"*

"His dad? I don't know. Him and Kane had a massive falling out and all he told me was that his dad now lives in China or Malaysia? I don't know. Either way he's not in the UK and hasn't been for about five years."

Richard felt that they were finally making some progress. *"You mentioned other addresses?"*

"Yeah, Kane mentioned he had a couple more in Southampton and one up North, he told me nothing other than that."

Richard paused and re-read his notes. *"How old is Kane?"*

Dani answered his question with a question, *"Do you know how old Crash Holly was when he died?"*

"Who exactly is Crash Holly?" asked Richard.

"What about Test?"

Richard looked confused, *"What are you talking about? What test?"*

Dani smiled, feeling she was now dictating the pace of the conversation.

"Crash Holly and Test are professional wrestlers who have died. Kane had a chart hanging up in his bathroom with these names and the age at which they died. Every time he had a birthday, he would cross one off. The last two crossed off were Crash Holly and Test. Yokozuna was next, and he died at the age of 34 so I would say right now that Kane is around 36 years

old."

Richard stopped taking notes and looked at Dani, *"Tell me about this book?"*
"What do you want to know?"
"Did he write this?"
"Yeah, why?"
"I want to keep it. Take it with me when I meet up with some old colleagues who I believe can shed some light on this situation."

Richard managed a wry smile, *"If you are telling the truth and this book holds the key to understanding Kane, then I need to read it properly."*

Dani looked over at Harper but before she could say anything Richard asked a most ridiculous question.
"Are blind people scared of spiders?"

Dani screwed her face up and chuckled, *"What are you talking about?"*
"It's a simple question, are blind people afraid of spiders?"
"I, I guess not," Dani replied, *"Why is this relevant?"*

Richard began his explanation.
"It is suggested to us at a very early age that spiders are scary. Watch a cartoon, and as soon as a spider is introduced it generates fear. Spiders are creepy. The eight long, thin legs. The speed at which they move, and the way they always seem to appear in horror

stories right alongside rats and snakes. You don't see many hedgehogs in horror films, do you?"

Dani felt like she had joined a brand-new conversation that she was not initially a part of but was expected to have some opinions and input.

"No, but sorry. I don't understand what is going on."

Richard continued, *"I think Kane is the spider. He has spun you many a yarn and now you believe he is a killer. You believe that this book contains the blueprints to these murders. He has played you. He has manipulated you and created this false identity just so you would love him and stand by him."*

Dani shifted her position in the chair and began to look quite uncomfortable, Richard continued.

"You were the missing piece. You were the putty he could mould and shape the way he wanted. He fed you lie after lie and over time, you believed it. You became convinced he was the monster he claimed to be, but he is just a spider. A small and creepy little thing, that is a lot weaker than you believe. Stand next to a spider, it's tiny, yet you allowed this tiny thing to control you. Blind people are not afraid of spiders because they do not buy into the lie. Without sight they can see more clearly than we ever could."

"Dad," Harper tried to get his attention, *"Dad! Is this relevant to anything? It's been a long day and I don't know if we're getting anywhere with this."*

"Harper, everything is relevant. I asked the question because I want your friend..."

Dani interrupted, *"Um, I think the word you're looking for is **girl**friend."*

*"I want your **friend**,"* continued Richard, *"to understand that she is not here providing me with answers to these killings but instead is showing me that she is someone that has been manipulated by someone else a lot smarter than her, and when he got bored, he moved on and dumped her."*

Dani jumped out of her chair.
"He dumped me! You know nothing. Stop jumping to conclusions that don't fucking exist."
Richard was quick to respond, *"So how did it end?"*

Dani knew the words that were to follow were not words she could ever take back, but they needed to be shared.
"Because he wanted me to get a tattoo." she sighed.
Richard laughed, *"He wanted you to get a tattoo. Stone me! That's the reason to break up with someone is it?"*

"You know nothing, you washed up old prick." shouted Dani as she lunged toward Richard.

*"Kane wanted me to get the words **I CONSENT** tattooed across my stomach so when I died, he would have permission to fuck me. Now do you get it?"* Dani leaned ever closer to the old man's face, *"He wanted to fuck my dead body and the tattoo, in his warped little mind, acted as a fucking permission slip. He wanted me dead so he could fuck my cold, dry pussy*

and produce an army of dead babies."

Harper stepped in between them and dragged Dani away. *"Bye Dad. I think it's best we go for a walk."*

Richard didn't respond as he watched his daughter take her lover by the hand and drag her out of the front door.

What had he just been a part of? What had he witnessed?

For the next few minutes, he sat in silence, dissecting every piece of the conversation with Dani, and trying to draw conclusions.

Richard knew he couldn't do this alone. Pulling the phone out of his pocket he called the one person he trusted.

"Hello Clara, it's Richard Neith. I need to speak to you as a matter of urgency. Can we meet tomorrow morning? It's regarding the Alphabet Killer. I have someone I need you to meet. Text me when is good for you. Thanks Clara."

ACT III

Outside, Harper and Dani hadn't ventured very far when Harper realised, she didn't have her bag. *"Shit, I need to go back in."*
"Why?" asked Dani.
"My bag. I need my bag. My phone and money are in there."
Dani threw her head back and glanced toward the heavens. *"Fuck sake. I'll wait out here for you."*

Harper slowly knocked the door. Richard answered. *"I forgot my bag."* said Harper, pushing past her dad.
Richard closed the door.
"What are you doing?" asked Harper, *"I'm going back out."*
"Tell me about Dani." replied Richard.
"Tell you what? I've told you enough about her, haven't I?"
"No, I want to know how you met. Why her?"

Harper threw her arms up in frustration.
"Why her? What do you mean by that?"
"Of all the girls in the club that night, why did you choose Dani."
"I didn't choose her, she chose me."

Harper thought back to that night they first met

and smiled.
"Yeah, she chose me. I felt incredible because I thought she was stunning. Short black hair, red lips, and the way she looked at me made me feel like I was wanted."
"Did you meet up after the club?"
"We had breakfast."
"Oh?" replied Richard. His eyes flicked to the right as his eyebrows gently lifted. *"Oh!"*
"It wasn't like that."
"What was it like then."
"Yeah ok, it was like that. She stayed the night. Big deal."
"It is a big deal. You take home the first girl you meet in a club..."
"No, Dani was different. I'd never slept with a girl on the first date, but she managed to, change that."

Richard huffed and shook his head.
"Look, she captured my imagination. Made me curious."
Richard laughed at what Harper had said. "Any more quotes from the Mills & Boon back catalogue? Grow up and see what is really happening here. She is playing some kind of game with you."

Harper bit her lip knowing that her father was not going to stop talking any time soon.
"The fact that there is a demented killer on the loose has ignited whatever mental problems she obviously has and sure, she is a very attractive girl but you, you are smarter than this. How can this book be the killers, how to guide or whatever it is, and she keep it quiet for

so long? It makes no sense. Can't you see?"

"You finished?" asked Harper. *"Now it's my turn. I came here to ask for your help. She needs your help. I need your help yet all you've done is create this divide between us and not take any of it seriously."*

Richard stood tall, towering over Harper.
"Listen to me. I am taking this very seriously. Even you must see that this is all very unlikely."
"Unlikely yes, but not impossible." Harper replied.

Richard shook his head.

"Will you stop shaking your fucking head at me." yelled Harper.
"I get it. I'm a big fat disappointment to you, well you know what. I'm not too thrilled about the way you turned out either."

Richard was taken aback by this sudden outburst.

"I know you would rather have Astrid here with you, wouldn't you? But she isn't here is she, Dad. No, she is living somewhere in Africa or wherever, married to a doctor and raising a lovely little family. I'm sorry Dad, but you are stuck with me. Your little lesbian failure who obviously has a taste for crazy bitches. I'm not going away until this is sorted, and it will get sorted."

Richard stepped away from Harper and sat back in his chair. Through narrow eyes he looked at

Harper. She is angry, but also scared.

"You not going to respond? At least show me a little bit of respect."
Richard continued to look at her but not speak.
"You're pathetic. I can see why Astrid left. Why mum left."
"I think you had better leave," Richard said in a soft yet firm tone, *"before you say something you'll later regret."*
"Don't worry, I was just thinking the same thing."

Grabbing her bag, Harper stormed out of the house and met up with Dani, who was sat on the grass verge.
"You ok Harp?"
"No. Can we just, walk." replied Harper, her voice trembling.
"Where?"
"I don't care. I need to be away from that bastard. When we get back, we will pack up and head home, to London. This was obviously a mistake."

Dani stopped and grabbed Harper's arm.
"We can't do that. We need his help. We need him to do whatever it is that people like him do."
"What?" said Harper
"I mean. You told me to come here and here we are. I don't like your dad but if he can help then I think you need to go back and apologise…"
"Apologise? What for?"
"You didn't let me finish. Let's carry on walking and

talking. At least that way we can burn off some of this anger and come back with a clearer head."

Harper took in a heavy breath, *"I have nothing to apologise for."* she said as she walked away.

Dani took a couple of quick steps to catch up with her.
"I know but I think this time you just need to be the bigger man. Apologise and then we can start over. I know men like him need to feel that they are in control. Let him have that moment and once we have what we came for we can move on and cut ties with him."

Harper stopped walking. *"Cut ties! Don't you think that should be my decision."*
"Yes sorry." Dani slipped her hand into Harpers. *"I'm sorry."*
"Can we just walk but no talk."
Dani smiled gently, *"Yes of course."*

ACT IV

7:13pm. Richard is pouring himself a second glass of whisky. Dani is in the bathroom and Harper is sat in the living room.
"What are you drinking?" asked Harper.
"It's a single malt whisky from Scotland. Ten years old and is, a thing of beauty."
"Ah, great." Harper had no idea what he was talking about, but small talk was about all they could manage right now.
"Dad, I'm going to go and make me and Dani some food. Did you want anything?"
"No." replied Richard.

Harper left the room to rummage through the kitchen and see what she could create for a late dinner.
"Where's Harp?" Dani asked as she came back to the living room.
Richard sipped gently from his glass before replying, *"I don't believe anything you said. I think you're a compulsive liar and that this Kane character is you."*
"What horse shit is this? How dare you!"
"How dare me? You're having a laugh at my expense. This is all your doing. Harper was happy before she met you. Now look at her, she is a mess, and it is all because of you."

From the kitchen, Harper could hear voices being raised once again. Her head dropped as she wished they would both stop fighting.

"You've got a screw loose and that beautiful girl in there, you don't deserve her."

Dani screamed and stormed into the office, slamming the door.

"What is going on?" asked Harper.

Richard nodded toward the office door.

"She, well, she has lost it. All I did was ask her if she was eating with you and she went crazy."

"I don't understand. Are you sure?"

"I haven't moved. I'm still holding my drink." Richard walked toward Harper. *"She needs to be left alone. Give her time to calm down."*

"Dani! Dani, are you in there?" Harper tried to open the door. *"Is this locked? Why is it locked!"*

"She's locked it from the inside. It's the only key I have so we have to wait for her to come out when she is ready."

"Dani please. Answer me." begged Harper.

"Leave her. Give her time. It's been a tough day for all of us."

Harper knew he was right. *"Come out when you're ready Dani, I'll be here."*

Sitting down, she clasped her head in her hands. *"What am I going to do?"*

Richard sat next to his daughter, *"Do about what?"*

"What am I going to do about Dani, Kane, this

whole situation!"

Richard held his daughters' hand, *"The only thing you can do right now is, nothing. Let her gather her thoughts together and once she feels comfortable, she will come out and we can discuss our next steps."*

Harper knew this was the right decision, but the feeling of immense guilt and frustration was difficult to control.
"What do you need?" Richard asked.
"I don't know. A drink would be a good start though."

Harper stood up and walked out into the kitchen. From the comfort of the settee, Richard saw a light come on, then off, followed by the sound of metal hitting glass. Harper walked out of the kitchen holding two bottles of lager.

"I'm going to chill upstairs for a bit. Is my room..."
Richard smiled, *"Yes your room is still as you left it. Get some rest now."*

A couple of hours passed by, and Richard was snoozing in his chair. From behind his eyelids, he could see a shadow moving by the office door. Opening his eyes he saw Harper, sat on the floor next to the locked office door. He didn't say anything, he just listened.

"Dani, I know this has been a rough couple of days but it's for the right reasons."
Harper paused and finished the last of her drink. *"I

got you a beer, but it's gone now. It got warm. Dani, can you hear me."

No response, nothing. Harper sighed heavily, stood up and went back to the kitchen, only to return a couple of moments later with another two bottles.
"I got you another beer. It's cold. I got one for me and for you."

Harper looked at the floor. There was a tiny black spider walking past her foot. It went under the door, and into the office.
"Tell me what you see tiny spider," said Harper. *"Is she in there?"*

The minutes ticked by as Harper slowly made her way through the final bottle.
"You made such an impact in my life Dani, and I don't want to lose that. I don't want to lose you. Listen, if this is all too much then we can run away. My dad has money and I know he will help us out best he can. We could, we could go North for a couple of months and I'm sure by then Kane would be caught. We could leave an anonymous tip off about Kane then vanish and wait for him to get locked up. Once he's gone, we move back to London."

Harper knew this was going to be a one-way conversation, but it didn't stop her from trying.
"I hope you can hear me. It's late and I'm tired. I went upstairs earlier but fell asleep and somehow that has made me more tired than before. I've never liked tak-

ing naps," Harper chuckled, "You're the napper."

Picking up the empty bottle of beer, she held it to her lips, hoping to salvage a few final drops.
"You know, before I met you, I always thought I was happy, but you've shown me something new. From that first night at the club, I knew you were someone special but now I don't know."

Harpers shoulders sunk as she stared at the 4 empty bottles of beer.
"What have I done to you? Please talk to me. I love... I..." Harper stumbled over her words.
"I have never been in love. I often imagined what it would be like but never thought it would be this complicated, this difficult. Dani, please answer me."
Still no reply. Harper dropped her head and squeezed her eyes together as tight as possible in the hope it would make the tears go away.

   2:43am. Harper is asleep and curled up against the office door with four empty lager bottles lined up against the wall.
Richard leans against the office door, it's silent. The whole house is silent.

Richard liked the silent life. For too long he worked in the major cities across the UK and had grown to despise them. He was introduced to a world inhabited by the lowest of the low. The hookers, the dealers, the thieves, and the killers. The outcasts of society that were beyond help. Beyond saving. The best thing to do with these types of people was to allow them to fight and reproduce within their own circles and hope it has a smaller impact on normal society. Every now and then there would be a crossover and innocent people would be dragged into the mess, but they didn't stay for long. They were either killed or they would simply vanish, presumed dead.

As the years went by, delivering the news to a grief-stricken parent that their child had been found dead after a heroin overdose or raped and murdered became quite blasé. It was just another day.

Drug runners being gunned down. Sex workers being stabbed. Faceless criminals being tortured. Children being stolen. This became the norm. Thirty years of relentless hatred and violence does something incomprehensible to the average man, for Richard, it made him yearn for peace. He knew he was never going to change the world but if he could protect his family from this life then he knew it was all worth it. And no one was going to jeopardise that.

CLARA MARSH

Born in Stockton on the 14th of March 1976, Clara Cynthia Marsh was an ordinary girl in an ordinary town. Her parents liked ordinary. Ordinary was safe, secure, and never created problems. That was until the 19th February 1993 when Clara's closest friend was killed in a hit and run accident. Up until that moment, everything was ordinary. As the days turned to weeks, Clara watched on as the authorities were unable to find the driver of the silver Ford Fiesta. They did track down the owner who confirmed the car had been reported stolen some three days before the fatal incident.

The young, yet inquisitive daughter of two very ordinary parents who lived in this very ordinary town, could not understand why this man had got away with killing her friend.

14th of March 1996, on her 20th birthday she told her parents that she would be leaving Stockton and moving north to Sunderland to peruse a career in the police force.

In 2005 she was married, by 2009 she was divorced. In 2011 Clara achieved the rank of Detective Chief Inspector, and yesterday received a phone call from Richard Neith.

As Clara made her way South from her home in Edgbaston, she found herself reminiscing about her time working with *Dickie Neith*.
They spent three years working together in the Birmingham area, but their professional relationship was never put into doubt. Richard was a very serious person who had little time for extra-curricular activities and in time Clara began to understand him and no longer invited Richard out for drinks, and other social events. There were never any romantic intentions. Clara liked people and therefore by default, liked Richard.

When Richard ran into personal difficulties at home he disappeared and some fifteen months resurfaced as a Private Investigator, working out of the Swindon area. What happened to cause Richard to vanish like that was never discussed. Every now and then their paths would cross, but as always, it was purely professional.

Clara was interrupted from her trip down memory lane by her phone.
"Boss, I know you're not technically working today but I need to speak to you about something. Can you

phone me back when you're not driving?"
Clara was confused, *"I can drive and talk to you Shaun. I'm not holding my phone."*
"No boss please, can you just call me. Thanks." and with that, he hung up.
"Strange", muttered Clara.

Looking at the road signs she could see that the services were just a couple of miles away. In a few short minutes she had arrived, and called Shaun.

"Right Shaun I'm parked up. What do you want?"
"Can you talk now boss?"
"Yes! I've pulled into the services. What's so urgent?"
Without hesitation Shaun replied, *"Hereford. He's killed again and this time it's Hereford."*

Clara fell silent as she mentally mapped the area around her.
"Ma'am, you still there?"
"Yes, Shaun listen. I'm at Strensham services. M5 southbound. I want to know where Gloucester and Hereford are from my location."
"No problems, hang on a second... So, Gloucester is approximately 15 miles south of where you are, and Hereford, is about 23 miles east."

Clara thought for a moment, *"Shaun, I need you to send me everything you have on this alphabet killing spree. Dates, locations, victims, weapons used."*
"Like Cluedo." Shaun chuckled, then fell deadly silent.

"You quite finished? If you can't take this seriously then I would prefer to work alone."
"Sorry ma'am."
"Email me that stuff now and I'll pick it up when I get to Swindon which will be in about an hour. Don't let me down Shaun."
Before he could answer, Clara ended the call.
"Why so close?" she thought. *"Andover and Basingstoke were close then you moved all over the place and now you're killing close again."*

Clara returned to her phone.
"Shaun, don't talk just listen and do what I ask. Andover, Basingstoke, Gloucester and Hereford. Connect the dots on a map and then send me all the major towns and cities that are within a 20 mile radius of the shape you've created. Got that?"
"Can I talk now?" asked Shaun.
"Well…"
"Yes sorry." said Shaun, *"I got that. Will attach it to the email with all the other stuff on it about the…"*
Clara once again ended the call.
"Now let's see what you have to offer me Dickie. Next stop, Swindon."

7:53am.
Harper wakes to the sound of Richards voice as he gently shakes her shoulder.
"I need you to wake up Harper. We need to talk."
Harper sat up and immediately grabbed hold of the handle to the office door. It was still locked.

"I've made you a coffee and some toast. I need you to come and sit over here with me and I'll explain what is going on."

Harper stood up, stretched, and walked over to where her coffee was waiting.

"What is it," she asked.

Richard waited until Harper was seated. *"It's Dani. She's gone."*

"What? What do you mean, gone?"

"I went out this morning and noticed the office window was open, I peered through, and she wasn't there."

"Why were you outside?"

"I go out for a walk at 5am every morning. It's how I get the blood moving around my body and motivate myself."

"But I thought the window was locked?"

"It was, but you can unlock it from the inside. I'm sorry."

Harper stood up and rushed outside to the office window. *"Dad, help me up."*

Richard walked outside to where Harper was waiting.

"Lift me up and help me get into the office."

Lifting Harper was simple enough. She was slim and slipped through the open awning window without too much difficulty. Richard shouted through to her, *"The key to the door is on the table."*

Harper found the key but didn't unlock the door. Instead, she sat down at the desk and hoped she could see a note or something from Dani. But sadly, nothing.

The only thing that looked out of place was the footstool which was positioned below the open window.

"That's how she got out." Harper sighed. *"Dani, why did you run?"*

"Harper can you unlock the door please."

Once Richard gained access to the office he went straight to his desk. He opened the bottom draw and slammed it shut again.

"Bitch!" he shouted. *"Fucking bitch."*

"What's wrong?" asked Harper.

"That bitch girlfriend of yours has stolen my money. I had £2000 in an unmarked envelope, in this draw and now it's gone. It's fucking gone!"

"You saying Dani stole it?"

Harper hoped the answer was yes because at least that means Dani would be ok. She'd probably head back to London, get her stuff, and go into hiding for a few days.

"Well, it was here yesterday morning." Richard sarcastically replied. *"Where has she gone?"*

"I didn't even know she had gone before you told me, so how would I know."

Richard walked out of the office and out of the

house, slamming the front door as he left.

Harper went back to her now cold cup of coffee and toast. Cold coffee was palatable, but cold toast, not so much. Harper sat back and tried to work out what Dani would do with £2000. Would she run back to London or go into hiding?

Outside, Harper heard a car pull up and what sounded like an argument soon followed. From the window she could see her dad in a heated conversation with a woman.

Clara spotted Harper peering from the window.
"Where is she Harper? Where is she?"
Richard opened the front door and DCI Marsh went straight for Harper.
"Where is she? Two thousand pounds in her pocket and on the run. Where would she have gone?"
"I don't know. I've already told.."
"I don't care what you've already told Richard. I want you to tell me."
Harper screamed back in frustration, "*I don't know! I don't even know who you are.*"

Clara changed the tone of the conversation with one word *"Kane."*
"What about Kane"
"She has gone to him, hasn't she? She's too smart to have gone back to your London pad so she has returned to the only person she can trust. Kane."
"How could she. She doesn't know where he is."

Clara walked slowly toward Harper.

"Don't be so naïve. She knows exactly where he is. We cross referenced all of the information we have, and we have narrowed it down to three locations."
"Narrowed what down to three locations? What the fuck is going on!"

Richard joined the conversation.
"Kane is in one of three locations. She knows where. She has always known and yesterday almost slipped up, which is why we had the dramatics and now her disappearance."
"Ok, look hang on a minute I need to digest all of this."
Harper rubbed her hands through her hair. *"Who are you anyway?"*

"I am DCI Clara Marsh. Richard called me yesterday and asked for help in bringing in Dani."
Harper looked over at her dad.
"You fucking coward. You called the police and didn't tell me."
Clara glanced at Richard. *"Always the dramatic with you isn't it, Dickie."*

"Dickie," thought Harper, *"Only certain people use that name."*

Richard locked the front door and offered Clara a drink.
"Yes please, coffee, black."
Clara sat down and pulled out her laptop.
"For the sake of everyone's sanity I'm going to pretend we don't know the location of Kane or Dani."
"What do you mean, pretend?" asked Harper.

"Please sit down and I'll share some information with you."

Harper did as she was told and sat next to Clara.
"Long story short, Kane has struck again and this time it is in Hereford. Please read the following list and tell me what you know. Kane lives in one of these locations."

As Harper read through the list Clara, went into the kitchen to speak to Richard.

Salisbury
Winchester
Reading
Southampton
Aldershot
Cirencester
Swindon
Cheltenham
Ross-on-Wye
Stratford Upon Avon
Bath
Bristol
Oxford
Chippenham

Harper waited for Clara to return.
"Southampton. He lives in Southampton."
"And this is fact, yes?" asked Clara.
"Yeah." said Harper.
"I think he has a second property. Did Dani ever mention a second location?"

"Yeah," Harper chuckled.
"What's so funny," asked Clara.
"Nothing. I've been so stupid to trust her."
"The second property?"
"Yes sorry. She mentioned that he had other places in Southampton and somewhere else up north, but she didn't know where. None of these places are up north though."
"Travelling up from Southampton, everywhere is considered going north."

Harper nodded, *"Of course. She was telling the truth, but I wasn't paying attention."*
"Don't beat yourself up Harper. She's a smart girl. Richard, make the girl a drink, she deserves one."
"So where is he then?" asked Harper.
Clara pointed to the list.
"Anywhere here, but I think it's interesting that Swindon is central to all of the places he has killed."
Clara was quick to correct herself, *"Within the Andover, Basingstoke, Gloucester and Hereford region I mean."*
"You think he's here in Swindon?"
"I don't know Harper. This is where I need to get back to my team and work this through what we think his next steps are."
"So, did Dani trick me into coming to Swindon? Knowing my dad lived here and that Kane would be here? But hang on, what about Exeter and Doncaster? They are miles away." Richard placed a cup of hot coffee on the table. *"Thanks dad."* Harper smiled.

"We can't make too many assumptions at the moment Harper," said Clara, *"It's true that Exeter and Doncaster are far out of the area, but I think he has done that on purpose to keep us on our toes. I expect the next location to be miles away from here then he'll return to this location to carry out two more kills before shooting off again in a random direction."* Clara took a sip from her coffee cup. *"I will bet you dollars to donuts Kane is within twenty miles of us right now. He thinks he has outplayed us, but he is so wrong."*

Richard sat down and nodded toward Clara, who returned the gesture.
"So where is he going for the letter I?" Richard asked.
"We have Ilford, which is 79 miles away, Ibstock which is 85 miles, and Ipswich which is 126 miles. Using his flamboyance for extreme distances, I would say that he will be heading to Ipswich. Which could be where Dani is also headed?"

"Dani said..." Harper stopped and stared hard at the table. *"Dani said that she knew where he would be for J. The letter J."*
"Go on," said Clara.
"Jarlow or something. She said there were two places he could go. Jersey or Jarlow, but Jersey would be too difficult to get in and out of."
"Jarrow?" asked Richard. *"Do you mean Jarrow?"*
"Yes, that's it. You say potato, I say, Jarlow?"
Richard looked at his daughter. *"You look exhausted Harper. Get some rest today."*

"I can't. I need to find Dani."

Clara closed her laptop and stood up.

"Harper, this brings me no pleasure in saying this, but I am placing you under house arrest. I suggest you take a couple of days to relax and allow yourself to properly process the events of the past few days. I will pick this up and track down Dani and I believe Richard, is heading to Bristol to meet with a mutual friend of ours."

Richard raised an eyebrow, *"Yes, something like that."*
"But wait, hang on you can't do that. Dad tell her."
"Harper you need to rest," said Clara. *"I trust you to understand that and stay put for a couple of days and get your mind in the right place. Once I have news on Dani or Kane, I will be in touch as we may need you as a witness if this should ever go to court."*

"What?" Harper felt she was being bombarded with revelation after revelation. *"What court?"*
"Harper listen, I have to go. Can I trust you to stay put for a couple of days until your dad gets back from Bristol? If not then I will have to tag you and leave an officer outside, or worse scenario is I have you arrested and kept in a cell for…"
"Yes, yes alright. I'll stay put. As long as I have food and drink then I don't need to leave the house."

Harper felt mentally beaten and knew deep down that this was the best option. Let the professionals take over and accept the offer of tranquillity for a day or two.

Clara made her way to the door.

"Harper, I will speak to you soon, and Richard, can we speak outside please."

As Clara left, Richard looked back at Harper, *"Are you sure you're going to be ok?"*

Harper managed a sincere smile and nodded. *"Of course. And dad, I'm sorry."*

Richard didn't verbally reply but Harper knew his smile was genuine and that was enough.

As the door closed for the final time, Harper closed her eyes.

"Maybe if I keep them closed nothing else will go wrong."

She tried so hard to keep her eyes shut but her emotions were not going to allow her to ignore the pain she was in. No matter how hard she tried to fight, the tears found a way out and within a few seconds, Harper was broken. Clutching a nearby cushion she cried harder than she had ever cried before.

GALLOWS

Fifty minutes is the amount of time it usually takes for Richard to drive to Bristol. Today he drove a little slower, so it took a little longer. He used this time to think through everything that had been said over the past couple of days and to separate the facts from the fiction, but what were the facts?

If Harper was sat in the car, she would be repeating everything that Dani had told her; *Kane is the Alphabet Killer, Kane abused her, Kane wrote a book.* None of this is real evidence. These were Dani's words, not Harpers. Dani planted this seed and left before anything could be confirmed. Maybe there was some truth in what she said?

Richard arrived at the Hilton Garden in Bristol just after 3:30pm and had booked a room for one night. He grabbed his small overnight bag from the back seat of the car and made his way into the venue.

"Well, fuck me. There's a site for sore eyes. Dickie, it's been too long. How are ya?"

Sat near the reception desk was a face Richard

hadn't seen in years and one he'd wished he never had to see again. The two men shook hands.

"Brian, it's good to see you, I just wish it was under better circumstances."
"Nonsense. Ya get yourself checked in and I'll meet ya at the bar." Richard nodded as Brian walked off.

Brian Galloway, retired cop and living in a beautiful four-bedroom detached property somewhere around the Leigh Woods area of Bristol. He shares his life with his trophy wife, Champagne (yes that really is her name), her elderly mother and their five retired police dogs. He is also a totally corrupt asshole who was commonly known throughout the force as Gallows. He was nasty, violent and most of all, he was feared.

The home he lives in was built on dirty money. A police pension would never pay for the luxury he now enjoys. He knows the wrong people but mixes in the right circles and is applauded by the community for his generosity. If only they knew that every penny he donates, is off the back of someone getting screwed over. Brian was not a man to be trusted but those who deal with him, already know that.

Richard entered the bar and spotted Brian sat in the corner of the room with 2 glasses of whisky. *"Grouse!"* Brian said as he handed Richard a glass.

Richard took the offering, smiled, and sat down.

"I got ya message Dickie, what is this about the alphabet deaths?"

"The Alphabet Killer! A man called Kane Azika."

"I don't like to use the term killer as it suggests we're just looking for one man. Plus, who is Kane Azika? That name hasn't been mentioned before."

"You don't think these deaths are related then? The ones where the killer left a page from a book as a way of mocking the police."

"No, they are entirely related, but what I mean is, there may be more than one person involved in doing this. Not the alphabet killer, but the alphabet killers."

Richard took a sip from his glass and thought about what he had just heard.

"You think there may be more than one person involved in this then?"

"Wait," said Brian holding his finger in the air. *"Wait, let me just send this, quickly."*

"You done?" asked Richard.

Brian smirked, *"Good health to ya and yas own"* he said as he emptied his glass in one mouthful.

"Now, because of the first two kills I believe it is safe to assume that the killer is local to that area. Hampshire or Wiltshire most probably. First attacks were done on familiar ground. He then heads northeast to Cambridge. North again to Doncaster. Follow that by going cross country to Exeter, Folkestone and Gloucester. It

is then followed by a short journey to Hereford before shooting off cross country again to Ipswich, Jarrow and then we weren't sure after that. Kidderminster, Knebworth, Kettering. They're all small places and in relation to England, they are all pretty central."

"What do you mean by central?" asked Richard.
Before answering Brian called for another round of drinks.

"The triangles Richard. The fecking triangles. Andover to Basingstoke to Cambridge. Doncaster to Exeter..."
Richard interrupted, *"Wait a second. If you list three points on a map and connect them all, then of course it's going to make a triangle. What other shape would it create?"*

"Let me track back a little. Yes, three points joined together on a map will make some kind of triangle. I'm not thick. We have been following his movements for some time now and a pattern is emerging. The triangles he creates are quite thin, and what I mean by that is, take A, B and C for example. Andover and Basingstoke create a small connection with Cambridge being the longer distance and when connected the shape of the triangle is very thin. Same pattern applies to all of the other locations except for Doncaster, Exeter and Folkestone, and this is where the second person comes into it."

Brian nodded across the room to the barman to

suggest he wanted more drinks.
"C'mon Dickie. Will ya hurry up and drink!"

Richard picks up his glass and takes a gentle sip.
"You were about to tell me about the second person."
"The second person did the kill in Doncaster and left our first killer down south."
"What makes you so sure."

"The first six kills were either by hammer or by knife except for kill four, Doncaster. The woman was attacked in her home and thrown over her balcony. Six floors she fell and that's what killed her. She was not stabbed or smacked about with a hammer. Same thing happened in Jarrow. The young lad was thrown from a bridge after being attacked and was killed by an oncoming train."

"How do you know so much? asked Richard. *"I met with the police, and they only know about Hereford. How are you so far ahead of them?"*
"Clara. You met with Clara. How many eyes do ya think I have Dickie? Remember who runs the yard. I'm the top dog."

"Yes, you are," thought Richard. *"You're not just the dirtiest dog in the yard, but you're also the one with the loudest bark."*

"Now the lad who was killed in Folkestone was the son of a high-ranking senior member of the armed forces. This information had to be handled delicately and with a total lockdown on information sharing."

"Delicately. So, they asked for you?"

"Yeah, why? Don't ya think I can do delicate?" Brian roared with laughter. *"Ya always were a funny cunt Dickie. Now, the posh knobs wanted answers without it becoming front page headlines. Since that day, every murder linked to these alphabet pages has been sent through me and my team and we believe he is now up to the letter O."*

The barman arrived to remove the empty glasses and replaced them with two full ones.

Richard was shocked.

"Fuck me Brian. What aren't you reacting to this? You must know who it is."

*"Who **they** are Dickie. Who they are. This is not the work of one man. We have CCTV images from the bridge in Jarrow where the young man lost his life, and we also believe we have captured the killer on CCTV coverage in Exeter, and in Leeds. From what we can ascertain from this is, is there are two different people involved. Both male and both as sly as a couple of dirty ginger foxes."*

"So, what's the plan. What is the next move?"

"After Leeds we believed the killer would stay local to the area. He had just killed a young lady in her hotel room and set fire to the body. I think this elaborate stunt was done to regain media coverage as thanks to our work, we had managed to maintain a media blackout, but he had the audacity to pin the page from his book onto the outside wall of the hotel where it

was found by a member of staff once they had been evacuated. This was shared online long before the police were able to control the situation."

Richard reached under the table and grabbed his bag.
"What ya doing there Richard?"
"I need to show you something."
"Well can it wait. I haven't finished."
Richard smirked and lowered his head submissively, *"Sorry, yes of course."*

*"Ya sarcastic English prick. So, following the pattern, we decided that the next kill would not be too far from Leeds, and we narrowed it down to either Manchester or Macclesfield and instinct told me that he would not pick Manchester as up to this point he has avoided the major cities. A murder, all be it a rather nasty one, took place in Macclesfield and the alphabet page was given to police by an anonymous young man who said **a vulture had given him the page** after he killed his guy. The young man was later questioned but was unable to give us any new information."*

"So, this kid spoke to our killer. Not an actual vulture?"
"Apparently so but I am unable to share anymore on that."
"Oh fuck off Brian. What are you hiding from me?"
Brian didn't respond. Instead, he raised his hand and once again demanded the services of the barman.

*"Nottingham, Nantwich, Northwich and Nuneaton."
Brian continued, "At this point we were checking and double checking all CCTV footage from train stations, airports and at locations in and around the previous crime scenes. What we found was then sent onto the N locations we had shortlisted and waited.*
"Where did he go?"

"Well, this is where it gets interesting. Brian paused, to empty his glass. *"Ya see, he never arrived at any of the listed locations and instead made the kill in Newport on the Isle of Wight."*
"That's some 180 miles away. When was he in Macclesfield?" Richard was fascinated by what Brian had to say and felt his old detective instincts kicking in once again.

"August 27 and in Newport on September 13." replied Brian. The barman arrived with two fresh glasses of whisky and removed the empties.
"Is everything good here," asked the Spanish member of hotel staff.
"Yes, of course. Are ya putting this all on the tab?" asked Brian.
"Erm yes sir. Room one, one, three."
"Wait a minute," said Richard. *"That's..."*
"Thank you lad. Here's a tenner for your efforts." Brian handed the barman a crisp ten-pound note which was greatly received.
"Are you putting the drinks on my room?"
"What's ya point Dickie? Retirement not treating ya

well?"

Richard had no come back. The brash Irishman had got one over on him, and not for the first time.
"You were saying about the Macclesfield and Newport dates."
"Eh, there is a two-week gap between the attacks." replied Brian.
"So that leaves plenty of time to travel between the two locations."
"If you suggest he is working alone, then yes, but that would mean he would have to be financially stable and able to support himself."
"Couldn't he have a job as a contractor or carry an HGV licence?" suggested Richard. *"That would allow him to travel the country without raising suspicion."*
"That's a possibility but very unlikely. It would be easy to track his vehicle and we would have got him weeks ago. Now Dickie, I need a piss. Hurry up and drink will ya, I'll get another round on my way back and you can show me that thing you wanted to show me."

Richard thought about all the conversations he had had regarding the Alphabet Killer. Harper, Dani, Clara and now Brian. He was certain someone was lying to him, but who?
Also, how much was Brian keeping from him. How does he know about kills that Clara is so far unaware of? None of this added up. Clara was excited to find out about Hereford. Yet Brian knows that this killer(s) is up to the letter O.

"C'mon Dickie, I have drinks." said Brian, announcing his return.
"But, I haven't finished this one."
"Will ya hurry up then. I won't be sitting down until you finish."

Control. Brian loved control.
Richard finished his drink and as Brian sat down, his phone rang. Brian didn't speak but instead made grunting noises and stared at Richard.
Without breaking eye contact Brian switched off the phone, *"What ya playing at Dickie?"*

"I don't understand what you're asking me Brian." replied Richard.
"Yas had the police sniffing around ya home and then ya managed to lose a key witness."
Richard looked hard into the eyes of Brian. *"You know I've spoken to Clara but what else do you know. Who else have you spoken to?"*

"It doesn't matter," replied Brian. *"Were ya going to share this name with me in the hope I would leave happy after feeding you all the info I have. Well, I have had someone check out this Kane Azika, and surprise, surprise, he doesn't fecking exist."*

Richard sat back in his chair. *"Ok,"* he said, *"what now? Shall we keep on drinking. Same again?"*

Brian stood up *"I have better things to be doing with my time. I don't want to be sitting here listening to ya*

throwing names at me in the hope ya can get one last moment in the spotlight."
"What, are you leaving. You can't just get up and leave with no reason."
"Kane Azika. The man doesn't exist. Yas feeding me regurgitated shit Dickie."
"How's your boy?" Richard asked.
"What did ya say?"
"How's your boy. Is he well?"

Brian shook his head and let out a muted chuckle.
"Yas always been a bit of a prick Dickie. What do ya want?"
"Sit down Brian, let's talk." Richard nodded to the barman as Brian pulled his chair out and sat down. *"By talk,"* Richard continued, *"I mean you allow me to talk, and you listen. Can you do that? Oh, and as I'm now calling the shots you can turn that bloody phone off."*

Brian did not like being told what to do but knew he had been out manoeuvred on this occasion. Several years ago, Dickie saved Kennedy from drowning. Kennedy was Brian's youngest child and from that day Brian promised to help Dickie, should he ever need it. Today was the first time Dickie had mentioned the kid since it happened. Brian, being true to his word, kept quiet and allowed Dickie to make his point.

"My daughter has a new love interest, Dani Palmore, and I got to meet her under very stressful circum-

stances. It turns out she has filled my daughters head with the idea that she knows who this killer is and was once in a relationship with the man. Dani gave Harper a book to read that was allegedly written by Kane and a lot of the content relates to the way these deaths have played out."

Brian interrupted, *"But that doesn't mean shit. A book about a man killing people can be vague and interpreted in any way the reader wishes. Sounds like this Dani girl is still hung up over her ex and is trying to frame him, or she's just fucking mental."*

Richard ignored everything Brian said and continued, *"There is one chapter in particular that is almost the blueprint for these attacks."*
"Ok go on." sighed Brian.
Richard turned on his phone and opened the photo gallery.

"I took a photo of the pages so I could read them to you."
"What's in your bag?" asked Brian.
"Nothing."
"You were going to get something out of your bag earlier. What's in the bag?"
"Brian, shut up and let me speak."
Brian, leaned back into his chair and lifted the whiskey to his lips. *"Go on then, dazzle me."*
Richard began to read.

Alice Malice was the name of his wife

He sliced her open with his knife
She cried and whimpered for her life
But Zachary skipped away

Bobby Stocks had seen all this
He tried to help but instead he missed
A flying blade, a final kiss
As Zachary skipped away

"Hang on there Richard, are ya reading me a fecking poem?"
"Brian just, listen ok. Each verse is in alphabetical order and each person is harmed in some way by Zachary. Richard continued *"Craig Potato had a stammer..."*

Brian let out a roar of laughter.
"Feck off Richard. Close ya phone and get out of here. Craig Potato? Craig fecking Potato! Yas an embarrassment. I had respect for ya once when ya saved my boys life but now look at ya." Brian swallowed the last of his whiskey. *"Ya sitting in a hotel bar spouting crazy poetry all because ya dyke of a daughter is getting finger fucked by some silly bitch whose ex wrote a book. Retire Richard. Retire and never darken my door again, ya daft prick."*

With that Brian stomped past Richard and left the hotel. Richard looked at the small cube of ice floating in his warm whisky. *"Bloody hell."* he mumbled to himself, *"Maybe he's right. Maybe I am getting carried away with this. Reading too much into what is basically nothing."*

He picked up his phone and continued reading.

Craig Potato had a stammer
He tried to cure it with a hammer
This killing game is not all glamour
Is what Zachary used to say

His true first love was Dani Duck
Who loved to sing and loved to fuck
But then one day she was out of luck
As Zachary skipped away

Richard closed his phone and shook his head.
"What am I doing?"
Leaving the drink on the table he collected his belongings and made his way to his room.

Outside, Brian was on the phone.
"Are ya serious? Portsmouth. So where is O."

Richard held back and listened best he could through the slight opening in the window.
"Q. So going straight to R?
A large HGV rolled past and created enough noise that Richard couldn't hear what else Brian was saying.

Brian put the phone back in his pocket and kicked the air. *"Fucking hell"*
Richard continued to watch as Brian stood still, staring at the road in front of him.
"What have you just been told Brian. What have you just been told?"

For a split-second Richard wasn't sure if he should step outside and see what the fuss was all about, but he thought better of it. Continuing the walk toward his room, he was starting to feel the effects of the afternoon drinking session.

Once inside his room he threw his key card on the floor and collapsed face first onto the bed.

His afternoon nap was cut short as his phone began to ring. It was Harper.

Richard ignored the call. Not long after, the phone rang again.

"Leave me alone girl" He put his phone on silent and went to the bathroom.

When he came back, he noticed there was a text from Harper. ***Please call me.***

Richard reluctantly picked up his phone and made the call.

"Harper." There was no reply. *"Harper, can you hear me?"*

"Sorry dad, yes I can hear you."

"What did you want."

"Where's the book?" asked Harper

"What book?"

"You know the one. Portrait of Them."

"I don't know. I thought this was urgent."

"It is urgent, I want to know where the book has gone."

"I said I don't know. It was in my bag but turns out it's not. Maybe Dani took it with her when she left?"

"No, she hasn't got it."

"How do you know?"

There was a pause before Harper responded, *"Because, I just asked her."*

TAKE THE MONEY AND RUN

For Harper, it had been a ridiculous morning. To be fair it had been a ridiculous few days, so what happened next was to be expected, except it wasn't.

Clara was long gone, and Richard had left the house to head down to Bristol.
From her vantage point cradled between two garage roofs at the end of the Close, Dani knew that now was as good a time as any to get back to Harper.
She lowered herself slowly onto the ground and casually walked up the road toward the house.
It was quiet, so much so that it made Dani uncomfortable. Surely there must be someone spying on her, somewhere? As an act of caution, she pulled the hood up from her jacket to hide her face.

Although everything had settled down and everyone was out of the house, Harper didn't feel calm. A week ago, none of this existed. A week ago, she was in a fun and loving relationship. A week ago, she believed she had found someone special.

Now, she doesn't know what to believe.

Scrolling through the various streaming services Richard has subscribed to, Harper was trying to find something on TV that would allow her mind to be occupied for a couple of hours.

"Why is he signed up to so many of these?" Harper mumbled.

Eventually she settled on the film, Avengers Endgame. She'd seen it before, but it's easy escapism. Bold colours and big explosions, that will do. The film had barely started when there was a knock at the door.

The door knocked again. The curtains were closed so she couldn't look out of the window to see who it was, and she was pretty sure that her father never had visitors, but for the third time, the door knocked.

"Fuck sake." Harper grunted in frustration, stomped to the door and unlocked it.

"Dani, what the fuck!"
"Is your dad here?"
"No, he's in Bristol for a couple of days. What the hell is going on?"

Dani pushed her way past Harper. *"Shut the door, we need to talk."*

Harper did as she was told and followed Dani into the lounge.

"What happened?"
"Harp, darling, please wait a moment. I need to eat.

*Can you please make me a sandwich or something? I haven't eaten or had a drink since yesterday."
"Yeah ok. Sit down and I'll sort it."
"I'll sit down but not in here. I need the toilet."*

With that Dani vanished as Harper started collecting ingredients out of the fridge. In a daze, Harper began to immediately over think what had just happened.

*Why was Dani here?
How is Dani here?
What is going on?*

Harper closed her eyes and tried to find the logic that must be hidden somewhere within this mess.

"Thanks Harp, I am starving," said Dani as she grabbed the sandwich from the plate. *"What's in it?"*
"I don't know," replied Harper. *"I'm confused. I thought you left?"*
"Ham and more ham."
"What?"
"In the sandwich. It's all ham. Doesn't matter, I'm so hungry."
"What is going on Dani. I spoke to you for hours last night and you just ignored me, then at some point when I had fallen asleep you decided to sneak out and rob my dad in the process."

Dani did not reply.

"Please speak to me. The police are after you and they

said you went back to Kane. Is that correct?"
Dani continued to eat.
"Where have you been? Dani. Where the fuck have you been!"

Dani finished chewing and reached inside her jacket pocket.
"Here's the money I apparently stole. One hundred, twenty-pound notes. Two thousand quid. Count it if you want."
Dani threw the envelope onto the coffee table.

"Next. The police are desperate for direction. They have no idea what they are up against but won't admit it. That DCI bitch wants to get everything she can out of me, spin it so it looks good for her, which in turn helps get her fat ass further up the ladder to becoming the next commissioner of the Met, or whatever her agenda is."

Dani then let out the smallest of laughs, *"And Kane, you think I know where he is? Somewhere between Jarrow and Southampton. How's that!"*

Harper listened to everything Dani had just said but had a question of her own, *"Why did you run?"*
"I didn't," replied Dani. *"Your asshole of a father paid me to go."*
Harper stared hard, *"Say that again."*
"After I locked myself in the office, I could hear the argument between you and your dad and, an hour or however long it was after, I don't know, he came into the office."

"How, if it was locked."
"He unlocked it."
"I thought it could only be unlocked from the inside and the only key was in the office?"
"Nope. He came in and basically told me to leave."
"No, I need to know exactly what happened. I want the details, not headlines."
"Really?" asked Dani
"Yes. I feel like everyone is playing me right now so please, tell me what happened."

Dani sat forward in the chair and began.
"He walked into the office and told me to get out. He didn't believe a word I had said and even accused me of being Kane. He accused me of lying to you this whole time and that I am the killer everyone is looking for. Kane is a made-up character in my own head and in order to protect you, he wanted me gone."
"You're Kane?"
"Apparently, yeah." chuckled Dani.
Harper did not see the funny side of this, *"...and are you?"*

Dani raised her eyebrows, shocked a what Harper had asked her.
"Are you for real! How the fuck am I a serial killer? You're more likely to be him than me. I'm shorter than you, older than you and not as fit as you. So, Harper. I ask you this. Are you Kane?"
"This isn't even funny." Harper replied.
"But it is. That's the point I'm trying to make. Your Dad is up to something, or he's just lost the fucking

plot."

Dani jerked forward, out of her chair, *"Where's the book?"*
"I don't know. I thought you took it with you."
"Shit. I need it. Where is it?" Dani began to panic. *"It's the only copy I have. The only copy anyone has."*
"I'll look upstairs," said Harper.

Dani ran into the office and emptied every cupboard and draw she could find. No sign of the book but she did find a couple more envelopes filled with money.
"Ah, I'll have those." she said as she picked up the small white packages.
"I can't find anything upstairs…"
"Harper, we need to leave."
"What! Why?" Harper was ignored. *"Why do we have to leave?"*

Dani threw a holdall at Harpers feet.
"Fill this up with as much food and drink as you can carry. I'm going to get us an uber and then it's a quick ten-minute drive to the station. We will jump on the first train we see and then grab a hotel for the night. We have that money Richard gave me to fuck off with so, I guess we should spend it."

Harper looked down at the holdall and then back at Dani. She knew this was a now or never kind of moment. This is the decision that she'd either live to regret or the one decision that would set her free. Problem was, she still had no answer as to

why they had to leave so quickly.
Harper reached for her phone.

"Who are you calling? Harper, who you calling?" Dani was struck with fear but dared not do anything to antagonise the situation further.

No one answered, so Harper sent a text message and held the phone in her hand waiting for it to ring.
No words were exchanged between the two as the promise of a phone call created an unusual sense of tension.

The phone rang, Harper lifted it to her ear.
"Sorry dad, yes I can hear you."

"Where's the book?"

"You know the one. Portrait of Them."

"It is urgent, I want to know where the book has gone."

"No, she hasn't got it."

Harper stared at Dani, *"Because I just asked her."*

Harper immediately ended the call and smiled, *"Let's do this."*
Dani let out a scream of excitement, *"Give me your phone, I'll call an uber and you get the supplies."*

Two hours after the phone call with her father, Harper was laying on her back, staring at the ceiling of a hotel room in Reading. This was a £75 a night hotel but right now that wasn't an issue.

"How much did my dad pay you to leave? Did you say there was two thousand in the envelope?"
From the bathroom Dani replied, *"Yeah two grand but look in my jacket pocket. It's on the chair."*
Harper walked over and searched the pocket.
"More envelopes?"
"Yeah, open them. I have no idea how much is there."

Harper returned to the bed and shook out the contents of the envelopes.
"There's got to be at least another two thousand here I reckon. Let me count it."

Dani left the bathroom and saw Harper, crossed legged on the bed with a big grin on her face.
"Including the two thousand you already had there is another three thousand, four hundred here."
"You don't have to shout, I'm right here"
"Oh sorry, didn't realise." Harper smiled.
"That's ok, it's good to see you smile. So how much we got altogether?"
"Five thousand. All in twenty-pound notes and as far as I can tell, all completely legit."

Harper held up one of the notes.
"The Queen has never looked so beautiful."

"You hungry?" asked Dani. *"I'm hungry. Grab a handful of that money and let's head downstairs."*
"What should I do about my phone?" Harper asked.
"Leave it switched off," replied Dani. *"I'm the only*

person you need speak to plus he could track you if you have it switched on. Let's have him panic for a few days."

The food was good, but the wine was even better. The bed in the hotel room was even better than the wine, especially as Harper was asleep. She looked at peace, calm. These past few days have taken their toll and it showed.
Dani on the other hand was awake and staring at the blank wall in front of her. She felt tired but almost too afraid to sleep. She couldn't help but feel that there was more to be done, more questions that needed answering, but she needed to focus on what was important right now, and that was Harper. Thinking and more thinking was not going to solve any of the problems, so sleep was the best option.

◆ ◆ ◆

Forty-five miles away, Richard was working his way through a third large whiskey as he continued to tidy his office. Cursing *the bitch* who stole his daughter, and his money. What other explanation is there? Dani outsmarted him on this occasion, and Richard has never been gracious in defeat. Her hurled his glass at the wall, knowing he may have just lost the only family he has left.
He tried calling Harper and still no answer. Her phone was switched off, straight to voicemail.

Pausing for a second, he flicked through his contacts list and made another call.
"I need your help. My daughter has been kidnapped."

❖ ❖ ❖

6:44am. Dani was already awake when Harper opened her eyes, *"You stayed."*
Dani looked round, *"Of course. I'm not leaving you."*
Harper yawned and sat up.
"Do we have a plan for today?" she asked.
"Yes, and I've been thinking a lot about this situation and last night, when you were sleeping, I made a call to that Marsh woman and, we are going to meet with her today in Birmingham."
This was not the reply Harper was expecting to hear, *"Oh wow, really! Are you sure that's the right thing to do?"*
"I need to prove to you that I am serious, and the only way to do that is to answer whatever questions they have and to help put an end to this madness."

Harper put her arms round Dani, *"I'm really proud of you. You're doing the right thing. When we leaving?"*
"Let's get some breakfast first then we can head off."
"Deal."

10:06am. Food eaten, and bags packed. The station wasn't far from the hotel but there was no rush.

For the first time in days Harper felt at ease. Everything felt right. She knew the meet up with Clara Marsh would be a difficult one but that wasn't for a few hours. Harper wanted nothing more, than to enjoy the moment. This moment. A moment of…

"Oh shit, I am so sorry. Are you ok?" Dani had managed to knock an elderly lady off her feet. *"I'm so sorry, I wasn't looking where I was going. Are you sure you're ok?"*

"Yes, yes. Get off me." replied the old woman. *"Watch where you're going won't you. Other people use the station as well you know, you hussy."*

As the old woman hobbled off into the main hub of Reading station, Harper looked at Dani,
"What are you doing now?"

Dani was trying so hard not to laugh, *"Sorry Harp, I didn't see her. She… she…"*
It was no good. Dani broke out into fits of laughter and no matter how hard she tried not to, Harper could not help but join in.
"Hussy? What the fuck is a hussy?" roared Dani.
"Sshhhh, we're trying to be incognito."
Dani tried to muffle her laughter, "Sorry, hussy."

Harper smiled but refused to acknowledge Dani who was still stood beside her giggling.
"Focus, Dani. What platform do we need to get to?"

In a futile attempt to compose herself, Dani inhaled deeply through her nose, *"Sorry. Platform 8.*

Looks like the train is due in a couple of minutes."

Harper grabbed onto Dani's arm.
"Before we head down and get the train, can I just tell you that I feel so happy right now."
Dani smiled at Harper, *"Hussy."*
Harper laughed, *"Is this a thing now? You calling me Hussy. I don't even know what it means."*
"It means…" Dani paused, *"It means. I'm in love with you."*
"I, think I'm in love with you" Harper replied.

The platform announcement briefly penetrated their moment, their bubble, but Harper didn't mind. Birmingham is the next destination and one step closer to putting an end to all of this.

❖ ❖ ❖

Richard checked his phone.
"Finally, it's back on." he said to himself. *"Now all you got to do Harper is answer the bloody thing."*

Pressing redial over and over was proving to be a pointless task. Every time he called, it rang, and went to voicemail. It wasn't Harper declining the call as it rang for too long. Maybe she can't hear her phone or it's on silent?
Richard searched his office for his coffee, only to remember he never actually made himself one. He tried calling Harper again. The phone clicked, success!

"Hello."
"Harper, it's me. Dad. Where are you?"
"What, who is this?"

Richard did not recognise the voice talking back to him. *"Who are you?"* he asked.
"What?"
"Who are you? Are you with my daughter?"
"I can't make head nor tail of this…"
"Hello. Are you still there? Dani, is this you?"
"Hello, can I help."

Richard was confused. Now there was a male voice on the call.
"Yes. This phone belongs to my daughter. Can you put her back on please."
"I'm not sure the lady was your daughter sir."
"Who is this. What is going on?" Richard was getting irate.
"My name is Davis and I'm a guard here at Worthing station."
"Worthing? Is Harper with you?"
"Sorry sir I don't know who that is. An elderly lady passed me the phone and walked away. Perhaps your daughter dropped her phone or left it on the train. We get that sort of thing happening a lot."

Richard tried another line of questioning.
"Do you know which train the lady who gave you the phone got off of?"
"Sorry sir no. It could be one of three trains."

"Three? That's all. So where have they come from?"
"Sorry sir but there are proper channels to go through if you want to report something as stolen."
Richard had heard enough.
"Listen you lazy bastard, I want to report my daughter as stolen. Can you deal with that? Clearly not. Put me through to someone else who can."

The station employee had heard enough and slipped the phone into the top draw. He could still hear Richard shouting as he closed the draw shut. Adjusting his tie, he decided to go for a wander along the platform.

Maybe when he gets back, the shouting would have stopped.

AIDEN ELLIOT

"What time is Marsh getting here?"
Dani looked at the clock on the wall.
"She will be here soon. Just relax. Grab a drink from the minibar and chill yeah."
Ignoring her suggestion, Harper continued to pace the room.
"You sure you want to do this?"
"Harper! Can you stop pacing and stop asking me the same thing over and over. You were fine with this when we were in Reading and now you've gone all weird."
"I'm worried," replied Harper. *"What if they arrest you?"*
"Arrest me for what?" Harper do you know something that I don't?"
"No. It's just, when Marsh was at my dad's place, she said she was going to arrest you. I shouldn't even be out here with you. I was put under house arrest.
Dani chuckled, *"You know house arrest isn't a thing in this country, right?*
"What do you mean?"
"In this country they..."

Dani was unable to finish her sentence when the door knocked.

"She's here."

Looking through the spyhole she could see Clara Marsh. Dani looked back at Harper and with a wink said,

"Let's do this."

With her hand resting on the door handle, Dani knew that this would be the turning point. The moment when everything will change.

"Are you alone?"
"Yes. I told you, no one knows I'm meeting with you both today. Is Harper here with you?"

With a quick check of the corridor, Dani once again asked if Clara arrived alone.

"Yes. I already told you that."

Dani looked straight at Clara, *"Well you can't be too careful now can you."*

"Dani, let her in and let's get this done."

"Thank you, Harper." said Clara as she walked into the room.

"Right, so how do you want to do this?" Clara asked.

Dani locked the door to the hotel room.

"Phones off."

Everyone did as Dani requested and placed them on the table, except for Harper.

"Shit, where's my phone?" she asked.

"I don't know," replied Dani. *"Did you pack it when we left the hotel? Phone them when we're done and*

ask."

Clara sat down, *"Harper, is everything ok?"*
"Everything is fine." interrupted Dani.
Clara looked straight past Dani and asked again *"Harper, is everything ok?"*
"Yes of course, why wouldn't it be?"
"I've had a number of missed calls from your dad, and he's also left me a couple of voicemails in which he suggests that you have been kidnapped."
Dani laughed, *"What the fuck!"*
Harper quietly shook her head, *"No, everything is fine. Honestly."*

By this point the three of them were seated.
"Dani, I don't want to dictate this, so I just want you to talk. Tell me about Kane. In your words. Tell me what you know and how we can work together to end this."
"End what?"

What a curious response.

"Erm, end the killing. Find Kane before he completes the alphabet. Isn't that what you want?"
Dani was firm in her response, *"Listen Marsh, I'm doing this because I want Kane found. I want answers to questions that only I can ask him."*
"Ok, first off please call me Clara and second, what questions."
"Well Clara," replied Dani with a sarcastic tone. *"The question is, why me? Why did he have to drag me into his world and now, I've allowed it to come be-*

tween me and Harper."
On hearing her name Harper looked over at Dani.
"Don't make this about me."
"I'm not. It's just the way that this has gone means you are now involved."
"You involved me. You didn't have to, but you did."
"Sorry excuse me," Clara interjected, *"Could I get a glass of water please Harper? Thank you."*

Clara turned her attention back to Dani.
"Now tell me everything you know."
Dani inhaled deeply. *"The man you're looking for is called Aiden Elliot."*
Before Harper could respond, Clara raised her hand and shook her head.
"Dani, please continue."
"Aiden Elliot is his birth name. Kane Azika is who he thinks he is. I never knew Aiden, I only ever met Kane. Aiden is two people. Kane is the killer, but Aiden is..."

Dani paused as she tried to remember the point she was trying to make.
"There's a book..." Dani swallowed hard and looked down at the floor, *"...there's a book that Kane wrote, and he is playing out some of these chapters and actually making the kills in real life."*

Dani pulled the book out of her bag. Harper was stunned, *"You said you didn't have it."*
"Yeah, I did. Sorry babe."
Dani placed the book on the table in front of Clara.
"Portrait of Them?"

"Yes," replied Dani. *"Read this. It's pretty much a paint by numbers guide to the murders that have happened, like the stabbing at a protest. Hammer attacks, fake suicide. A-Z stuff. The fondness he has for Murder Day."*

Clara interrupted, *"Sorry, but what is Murder Day?"*
Harper returned with a glass of water and placed it on the table next to the book.
"This." Harper opened the book. *"Mr Dude Ray. It's a shit story about a guy who generates this kind of cult following online and at some point, in November, it's his anniversary."*
"When in November?" asked Clara.
"The eighteenth." replied Dani.
"How do you know that?"
"I've read this enough times to know what is what."
"So how does Murder Day tie in with what's been going on?"
Dani narrowed her eyes, *"What do you mean?"*
"You speak about Murder Day, but you haven't told me how this links to Kane. Or Aiden."
Dani puffed out her cheeks in frustration.
"Let me finish making my point, then you will see what it is I am talking about."

Clara picked up her drink with one hand and with the other signalled for Dani to continue.

"Kane had always been a problem from the first day we met but I couldn't help myself. I was so bored, and he was like a new toy. Problem was this toy had some

major faults. Physically he was in mint condition but mentally, there was a whole lot gone wrong. If you shook him, you'd hear all the pieces inside his head rattle. He didn't just have a screw loose; the screw had fallen right out."

"What are you trying to say?" Clara asked.
"He was mentally, emotionally damaged. Fucked up, retarded. I don't know how you want me to put this but if someone was going to go on a killing spree then it was going to be him."

"Why do you always speak so poorly of those with mental issues?" Harper asked.
Dani shrugged her shoulders. *"I don't. You just see the best in everyone and give these people more respect than they deserve."*

Harper was gobsmacked. Was this the same Dani that was with her in Reading that very morning? If so, why is she now acting like a total bitch?

"There's one story within the book which is titled A-Z, then GOD follows, and this is pretty much the whole thing. He talks about going on an alphabetical killing spree and how at the end he will be considered a god."
"But again, these are just the words of someone who, as you put it, is mentally unstable."

Dani stood up and looked out of the window. This was the first time she had ever visited Birmingham and after today, vowed to never come here again.
"I don't know what more I can tell you." Dani sighed.

"Can I take the book away with me and get my team to go through it?"

Dani's moment of reflection was shattered with this question. *"No."*
By this point Harper had sided with Clara.
"Dani, why not. This could lead to the arrest of a man that needs to be stopped."
Dani focused her aggression on Harper, *"Who's fucking side are you on!"*
"This is not about taking sides. This is about coming together to stop Kane. To do the right thing. Let them take the book. There might be things in there you've missed?"
"Things I've missed? I know that book. I have read every chapter repeatedly.
Domino Cortez, a story of revenge following years of abuse, Frank Hunt the Baby Sniper, Zangara..."

Dani stopped and took a deep breath.
"The boy was called Kane Zangara and he was Aiden's best friend. Zangara died when both boys were twelve and I don't think Aiden ever got over it. Following that he had his own issues with violence, like, it was like, it was following him around. There was violence at home, on the streets and even at school."

At this point Dani returned to her seat and sat down.
"Aiden became Kane after he attempted suicide. It was like his physical body survived but his mind was lost. Maybe on that day Aiden did die and, in his

place, stood Kane?"

Dani lifted her head to see Clara was reading the same story that Dani had just been talking about. She looked at Dani, *"I want to read this last part aloud if that's ok?"*
Dani didn't verbally respond, opting to gently nod her head instead.

> ***I think back to the time when I was
> twelve. He was also twelve.
> My friend Kane Zangara will no longer breathe
> but he will forever live through me.
> A family wiped away so quickly, without reason.
> Without an explanation as to why I lost my friend.
> My childhood. My parents.
> RIP Kane. I will be with you again soon.***

Clara closed the book.
"I'm taking this away and getting someone to piece it all together. If this book is as powerful as you're suggesting, then it should be enough to track him down. Correct?"
Dani nodded, *"But you can't take the book. It's mine."*
Clara stood up, *"Listen you're lucky we haven't arrested you. Others would have done so but I'm trying my best to trust you."*

And with that single statement, the tension in the room began to rise once more.
"What! I've done nothing but be cooperative. I came forward with this information. How does that mean I get arrested?"

Dani didn't get an answer to her question as there was a knock at the door.

"Fucking bitch, I thought you said you were alone?"
Clara ignored Dani, looked through the spyhole in the door, then unlocked it.
"What are you playing at," growled Dani.
As the door opened, a stout, red-faced, middle-aged man walked in.

"So, which one of ya is Dickie's daughter?"
Harper stood up, *"Why, who are you?"*
The man laughed, *"I'm an old friend of ye paps, so old in fact, I remember the night yas were conceived."*
With that he gave Harper a little wink.
Harper looked at Dani, *"What the fuck is this?"*

"May I introduce an old colleague of mine." said Clara. *"Brian Galloway, or Gallows."*
"Gallows! What sort of name is that?" chuckled Dani sarcastically.
"The sort of name that will land you in a whole heap of shit if you don't cooperate. Do you understand me girl."

A second man walked in holding a briefcase. He was younger, well dressed and would be considered the absolute in Mediterranean male beauty, if the circumstances were different.
"Any more coming in?" asked Dani.
"Drop the attitude girl. This is Gin, he's my wingman."

Gin glanced at Dani and placed the briefcase on the

table.
"I want you to get out of my room." Dani yelled. *"Both of you, get out!"*
Gallows closed, then locked the door.
"I'm afraid that's not going to happen."
"Brian, please sit down," said Clara as she gestured toward the empty seat.
"Thanks, Clara." Brian sat down and pulled the briefcase toward him.
"Dani we can do this one of two ways. My way, or the hard way."

Dani rolled her eyes.
"A little cliched isn't it?"

Brian smiled, opened the briefcase, pulled out a bottle of Jack Daniels and a plastic cup.
Dani looked at Gin.
"So that's why you're called Gin, because you carry his alcohol around for him."
"No, I am called Gin because my full name is Giancarlo Domani Calabrese, but it is easier to say Gin."
Dani smirked, *"He's cute, and funny."*
"So, as I was saying, my way or the hard way."
Dani shook her head, *"Whatever, yeah."*

"Good, we will do it my way." Gallows poured himself a couple of shots of Tennessee's finest and continued.
"I will ask ye a question and ye will answer it. Gin is recording this conversation and when we have Kane, ye will be arrested."

"Hold on," said Clara, *"the idea was for you to support me, retrieve the information we need then to allow Dani and Harper into my custody for the duration of the trail and then after there was to be a discussion regarding Dani's role in this. We never agreed she would be nicked now."*

"She won't be nicked now, but once Kane is arrested then her time will come. Now please let me continue." Gallows took a swig from his cup and looked at Dani. *"For the purpose of this recording, what is yas name."*
"Dani."
"Yas full name."
"Danielle Brooke Palmore."
"Do you believe you know the identity of the Alphabet Killer?"
"Yes."
"What is his name."
"Aiden Elliot, but you will know him by the name, Kane Azika."

Harper leaned back and carefully watched Dani. *"Every time she opens her mouth there's a new revelation about Kane. How many more secrets is she hiding?"* Harper wished she could voice her concerns out loud but now was not the time.

"Aiden Elliot ye say. That would explain why this Azika name never showed up on our records." Gallows scribbled something down on his scrap of paper

then continued. *"Is Aiden Elliot his birth name?"*
"Yes."
"How do ye know this man?"
"We dated."
"When."
"In the past."

Gallows took a quick sip from his cup.
"Don't get smart girl. When in the past did yas date?"
"What is yas?"
"I'll ask one last time..."
"Ok yeah I get it. We dated for a couple of years but broke up about two years ago."
"Where is he right now?"
"I don't know, Southampton probably or up north."
"Where is he going next?"
"What do you mean?"
"P. Where is he going for P?"
Dani shook her head, "The toilet?"
"Don't get too fecking confident girl. Yas already testing me."
"Don't ask me stupid questions then about where Kane is going to being pissing."

Gallows leaned forward, *"P. The letter P. Ya know where he is going, and I need to know."* he whispered.
"I don't know where he is going or where he has been. I haven't spoken to him since we broke up. And nothing has been said in the news or anything about him being that far into the alphabet."

Gallows took another, larger sip and continued his

questions.
"Does he have any immediate family?"
"Not that I know of."
"Any kids."
"See previous answer."
"Does he have any hobbies?"
"What, aside from all the killing?"

Harper whispered, "Dani, please don't."
"Sorry but this is ridiculous. What hobbies does he have? Why are you asking me that? Do you want to catch the guy or date him?"

Clara spoke up, "Dani, we need to build up an idea of who Kane is and put all this together to get a better understanding…"
"The girl knows what she's saying Clara. Don't waste your time."
Dani glared at Brian. "*The girl!*"
"Yes, the fecking girl. Now answer the god damn questions!"
"No one asked you to be here."

Brian turned to Clara, "I need a piss. Sort this out or I'm gone."
As the bathroom door slammed shut Clara looked at Dani.

"*Brian may be a bit of a prick, but we need to keep him on our side. Believe it or not, he can be really useful when used correctly.*"
Dani held her lips firmly closed and grunted though her nose.

Clara nodded, *"Good."*

"What about him?" asked Harper.
"Gin? He's harmless. Does what he's told, never asks questions and basically is a real waste of space, but Gallows keeps him close for whatever reason."
"He can hear us, right?"
"Oh yes I can hear you. I just don't care about what it is you are saying. I am paid to listen, but not to you."
Clara raised her eyebrows, *"And there you have it. He listens, but he can't hear you."*
Harper chuckled.

"What's so funny." asked Gallows as he walked back into the room.
"Nothing really, we were just talking to your man, Gin."
"Yeah," replied Brian, clearly unimpressed, *"talking, were you?"*
"Only enough so they could hear me."

Brian laughed and slapped Gin on the shoulder.

"Love this fecking man. I never understand what he's talking about but he's loyal and don't ever underestimate someone who shows loyalty."
Dani looked at Harper, smiled and nodded.

"Now, Danielle Brook Palmore, I want to tell ye a wee story about a young girl who thought she was able to outsmart a wise old detective, but she hadn't figured on him being the wise old dog that he was."
"Is the girl in the story me by any chance, and the fat old detective. Could that be you?"

"Yes indeed. Ye must have heard this one before. It's a real corker. The little girl thinks she is all that and wants to turn this all into a game, but the wise old detective has played these types of games before. He always wins, and the sooner the girl and her soppy pillow princess accept this, the easier everything will be."
Harper stands up and attempts to leave. *"I'm done with this."*
"Where are you going?"
"Outside, where I won't be subject to this type of rubbish. How do you get off talking to people like this!"

Gin stepped in front of Harper, blocking the entrance.
"Sorry girl, yas won't be leaving." said Gallows as he pointed back to the bed. *"And for yas information I will talk to whoever, however I wish."*

Harper looked at Clara.
"You can't keep me in here against my will."
"Sorry but we have to." replied Clara, *"This has become a major investigation as you are about to find out."*

Gallows faced Clara. *"What the hell you on about. You want **me** to tell her?"*
"Tell me what?" asked Harper.
"No not ye," replied Gallows, *"Yas little tart over there."*

Dani glared at the old man sat opposite her but said nothing.

"Ok so, I'll tell yas where we're at. Kane is now responsible for eighteen deaths."
"What." Dani was shocked. *"What do you mean eighteen?"*
"Eighteen, yas know. The number after seventeen but not quite nineteen."

Dani didn't respond.
"We had a report of a murder which fits yas man. A young girl and the obvious alphabet book page."
"A young girl?" Dani replied. *"How young are we talking here?"*
"Young enough."
Dani figured that for now, that was about as much information she was going to get out of the Irishman.

"Eighteen, so he's up to the letter R?" suggested Harper.
"No, he's done R, so next would be S, and I assume that would be Southampton."
"Where was R?"
"Rochdale."
Harper leaned over and added her own opinions.
"Why would you assume that S is going to be Southampton? He's hardly going to shit on his own doorstep now is he."
"Harper," shouted Gallows, *"This has sweet F A to do with ye right now. Keep it quiet because I believe we are in the same room as Kane himself."*
Dani looked up.
"What me? What is it with you old men thinking I'm a

155

serial killer? Kinky fuckers."

Brian grinned as he felt Dani was lowering her guard.
"I don't think Kane was working alone. The kills between the north and the south of the country have a distinct pattern and, how can I put this? Let's just say, for the benefit of the stupid, he hasn't covered his tracks as well as he thinks he has."

"Fuck my life! I had this same conversation with that dick down in Swindon and I'm fucked if I'm going to go through it again. How the hell could I have been a part of this. I've been with Harp for the past, however many weeks."
"You have vanished on a few occasions though."

Dani turned her head and looked at Harper. *"I beg your pardon?"*
Harper repeated herself, *"You have vanished for a day or so a couple of times, and I've never been able to get hold of you."*
Dani shook her head in disgust and looked back at Gallows.
"What do you want?"

"I want ye to surrender that book. I want ye to stay here tonight, and I want ye to report to the station tomorrow to assist in a live televised appeal."
"Appeal? What appeal?"

"Tomorrow at 5pm we will go live across the web with an appeal which will bring Kane front and centre."

"But this is what he wants. He wants the media attention."

"I know and hopefully this will prevent him from completing the twenty-six. His obvious arrogance will be his downfall and that's when we will strike. We can't do anything about those who have already died but we can prevent any further loss of life."

Dani thought for a second as she weighed up the options in her head.
"What if I don't agree to it?"
"Then it's simple. Yas be immediately arrested, and we will proceed with the appeal as planned without ye."
"So why do you need me to be there?"
Gallows leaned forward, *"Because I don't fucking trust ye."*
Dani moved her face away as the stink of whisky flowed out of Brian's mouth. Looking over at Clara, Dani asked if this was something Brian was allowed to do. Keep them locked up in a hotel. Clara nodded.

"I can fecking do what I want, and I will do what I think is in the best interest of this case, and there is nothing Clara or anyone else can do about it. I am leaving now and there will be an officer outside your door so don't try anything stupid. Gin will be back tomorrow at 3pm to pick ye up. Any more questions?"

"Yes," If I'm Kane, why do I need to be at my own appeal?"

"We will all find out tomorrow now won't we. Clara, thanks and I will see ye tomorrow. Goodbye."

Dani got up and walked to the bathroom, slamming the door shut behind her.
"What the hell was that all about?" Harper asked.
"As I said earlier," responded Clara, *"I have known Gallows a long time and if there is someone who can get this done then it is him."*

Clara picked up her bag.
"Listen Harper, don't let Dani do anything stupid tonight. They have you both under surveillance and I'm sure you don't want Dani to be arrested when she is innocent."
"You believe she is innocent." asked Harper
"Well yes," said Clara *"don't you?"*

Two hours have passed since Clara left and it's been two hours since Harper and Dani spoke to each other.
"Dani we need to speak."
"Not tonight. Please. Today has been shit, so I just want to watch crap TV and sleep."
"Are you doing the appeal tomorrow?"
"I don't really have a choice do I."

On the other side of the door, they could hear the officer assigned to them walking away. Harper quietly crept across the room and peaked through the spyhole.
"Has he gone?" asked Dani
"The fat one has but they've plopped another one

there to replace him."

"Fuck this." Dani muttered as she threw the TV remote across the room. *"I'm going to sleep."*

Harper looked on as Dani curled herself up in the chair.

"You can have the bed."

Dani covered herself with a hoodie and closed her eyes. What started as a beautiful sunrise in Reading was ending as a miserable night in Birmingham. Harper made herself a nest of pillows and tried her best to relax.

Maybe tomorrow will be better. Maybe tomorrow this will all come to an end.

A IS FOR APPLE

I don't think the rain is going to let up anytime soon."
"That's ok Gin, yas not going yet anyway."
"Uh!" Gin turned to face Gallows. *"I need to go back home at some point. I have a family."*
"Do ya really! Funny as ye never seem to bring it up."

Gallows continues talking, but not once does he look up at Gin.
"What's more important to yas? This job or yas fecking family?"
Gin raised his brow, *"Well obviously..."*
Gallows cut him short, *"I need ye right now to do the following. I want a list of every location, every name, weapon used and where the alphabet clue was left."*
"But we did all this already."
"And now I want ye to do it again. We need to know exactly what we're dealing with tomorrow before we do this appeal. Get me that info and then we can discuss why ya hate yas job."
Gin was stunned, *"What? I don't hate..."*

Once again Gallows silenced him.

"What is it ya say? Stay zitto e lavi, or somethinglike that?"
"Stai zitto e lavora stronzo."
Gallows chuckled, *"Funny language, now do some work."*

Gin sat at his desk and glanced at the photo of his wife and new-born daughter, Liliana. Feeling a sense of guilt, he lifted the picture frame and placed it face down.
"I'll be back in an hour or so and I want that information ready for me when I do."
"Where are you going?"
"Who the feck are ye? Me mother! Ya funny twat, now get the work done."
"Stronzo." replied Gin.
Gallows slammed the door shut leaving Gin in the empty room with nothing to keep him company except for the humming of the computer and the ticking from the clock on the office wall.

When Gallows returned, he saw Gin looking out of the window.
"Yas better have done the work rather than just standing there gawping out of the window like a soppy dog."
"It's all on your desk. Can I go now?"
"No. Yas can go when I say so."
Gallows sat down and read through what Gin was instructed to do.
Twenty minutes passed.
"Ok so, yes this is excellent. Go home now."
"Thank you." replied Gin.

"I want you at the hotel for 10am to collect that Dani girl and bring her to the station. Me and Clara will meet ye there."

Gin didn't respond. Instead, he looked up at the clock, shook his head and walked out.

◆ ◆ ◆

9:03am.

"Did you sleep ok?

"As best I could I suppose, considering."

Harper pressed her lips together and offered a gentle smile.

"Are we ok?"

Dani nodded.

"Of course. Yesterday was shit, but we knew that was going to happen. Just didn't expect that Irish bloke to turn up with his Italian monkey butler."

Harper kissed Dani on the forehead. *"Coffee?"*

"I will in a minute," Dani replied. *"I want to grab a shower first."*

As Dani disappeared into the bathroom Harper did consider joining her but thought better of it. She needs her space, and although a great stress relief, sex is probably the last thing on her mind right now.

"Dani, when you've finished, I think we need to sit down and talk. I know I sound like a broken record but... I'm not sure what I'm saying... All we do is talk.

How many more times do we have to talk?"

A few minutes later Dani opened the bathroom door.
"Wow." whispered Harper, *"I forgot how good you look naked."*

Dani leaned against the doorframe.
"Can we talk later?"
Harper smiled and made her way towards Dani.
"Of course, anything you want."

It was at that point the door knocked.
"Hello, excuse me."
Dani grabbed hold of Harper, *"Ignore it."*
Harper did as she was told and slid her hand down Dani's back. Her fingers gliding across Dani's wet skin and down toward her bum.

"Hello, excuse me. I'm coming in now."
The door clicked open and in walked Gin.
"What the fuck man," screamed Dani as she stood naked in front of the Italian.
Harper pushed her into the bathroom and closed the door.
"You can't just barge in here like that. Who the hell do you think you are! You have no right to walk in uninvited and gawp at my girlfriends naked body."

Gin held up his hands waiting for the shouting to stop. Once Harper stopped, Gin seized his opportunity to explain what was happening.
"I was told yesterday to collect Dani at ten and bring

her to the station for a briefing, before the appeal this evening."
"But that's not until five."

Gin was apologetic, *"I know. I'm just doing what is asked of me. I'm sorry."*
"Why are we going so early?" Dani asked as she walked out of the bathroom. A white hotel towel hiding any further embarrassment.

"I've been told you need to be at the station now. Gallows needs to speak to you before the appeal."
"That's seven hours away."
"Look, I'm sorry. I am just doing what I am told."
"Hang on," said Harper, *"Is it just Dani who is going? What am I to do then? Sit here in this room all day"*

Gin began to rub his eyes in frustration.
"I don't know how many times I must ask. You need to come with me now to have a meeting with Gallows and Marsh before the thing you are doing this evening."

Dani let out a scream of frustration as she went back to the bathroom.
"Now what is she doing?" asked Gin.
"I'm getting dressed you prick." Dani shouted from the bathroom, *"Is that ok?"*
Gin walked out of the room and into the corridor.
"I will wait for you here."
"Yeah whatever." replied Dani.

Harper walked over to Gin. *"I'm coming with you,"*

she said sternly.

"No, my instruction is only to bring Dani."

Harper shook her head, *"No, this isn't up for debate. I am coming with you, or I'm going to lock this door and make this as difficult as possible for you."*

Gin laughed, *"Why is everything so hard all of the time with you people. Ok, yes let's do that. It sounds great."*

Harper went back into the room and packed her bag. Outside she could hear Gin mumbling something, probably in Italian and probably none if it particularly friendly.

Twenty-Five minutes after Gin had picked up Dani and Harper from the hotel they arrived at the station. A tall, thin, gaunt looking man in an old grey suit met them at the door and asked them to follow him to the briefing room.

Dani leaned over and whispered, *"He looks like English Slenderman."*

Harper laughed.

"Is something funny?" asked Gin.

"Yes, thank you." replied Dani.

Gin didn't understand the reply so didn't bother with a response, it didn't matter anyway, they were at the briefing room. Inside it looked strange. Big, empty space with just a desk in the middle of what would usually be the seating area. Around the desk were eight empty chairs and two that were occupied.

"Yas late." Gallows bellowed. *"I thought I told ye to pick the girl up at ten and why is Dickie's daughter here as well?"*
"My name is Harper!"
"I don't care right now." Gallows responded bluntly.
"Harper, Dani, please sit down." Clara was obviously playing the role of good cop today.
"Now the reason why I wanted you here so early was to go through and understand, not just what we are to be discussing this evening, but to also talk about those whose lives he took."

Dani was confused, *"Why? What's the point?"*
"I'll tell you why girl…"
"BRIAN! Please let me deal with this."

It is not often *Brian* gets shouted out and it's even more of a rarity for people to call him Brian.
"Ok Clara, yas have two minutes."

Gallows sat back in his chair, staring at the DCI.
"As I was saying, Dani, we have asked you here today to go through what we know about Kane and how we are going to structure the appeal this evening."
"You said something about those he killed?" asked Harper.
"Yes, we want to go through the list of people who were murdered by Kane. The Alphabet Killer."
"But why do I need to know who the victims were?"
"They were people Dani, not victims. I want to talk about the people."
Dani squinted and gently shook her head, *"I don't*

understand but yeah, whatever."

Clara nodded toward Gallows who then took control of the conversation.
"I want to know which of these people yas killed."
"Not this again." sighed Dani. *"I haven't killed anyone."*
"Well let's see shall we. Gin, switch on the screen and I'll go through what we have."
Gin walked over to the large plasma screen on the wall, switched it on and connected it to the waiting laptop.

Andover.

"Billy McKinnon, Male, 17 years old, killed in a fast-food restaurant toilet with a hammer. Previous, he'd been arrested twice for possession. Lived at home with his disabled mother in a council flat. He was small time so had no conflict or issues with rival gangs.
The page was found on the floor of the toilet. Soiled and damaged by the attack so we can assume the page was dropped before or during the murder."

Gallows clicked through to the next slide.

Basingstoke.

"Richard Farnell, Male, 31. Stabbed to death in the Festival Place car park in Basingstoke. At the time of the attack, he had just finished a phone conversation with his brother who lives in Dublin. The conversa-

tion ended at 10:20pm and he never heard from him again. Time of death is estimated to be just after that at around 10:25pm.
The page was found on the floor of the car park. The letter B."

Clara lifted her hand to stop Gallows.
"May I add that at this point there was no need to match both attacks to each other as the boot prints found at both locations were of different sizes."
Dani smirked.
"What's so funny?" asked Gallows. There was no response.

Cambridge.

"Rebecca Collingwood, 33. She has two daughters and a husband. She comes from Hardwick and is a part time charity event planner. Mrs Collingwood was stabbed during an environmental protest at Kings Parade which she had attended with two of her friends and her 14-year-old daughter. It appears to be a totally random attack and sadly a case of wrong place at the wrong time. A weapon was retrieved at the scene from an attendee's bag. We believe the knife was dropped there on purpose in an attempt to throw us off the scent and slow us down."

"Did it work?" asked Dani.
"Yas tell me." Gallows replied.

Doncaster.

"Edwina 'Winny' Shaw. Female, 71. She was attacked in her home and thrown over the balcony. She fell from the sixth floor and was announced dead at the scene. She lived alone but was a very popular member of the community. There is CCTV from inside the block which shows a man speaking with Ms Shaw, but the man was never identified by anyone and was never seen leaving the building."

"What do you mean?" asked Harper.
"We have a male talking to our victim both outside and inside the building. He never enters the lift with Ms Shaw, and we never see him leave the building. The only possible option is he left via the stairwell where there is no CCTV coverage."

"I'm sure people use the stairwell all the time. You can't treat everyone who used the stairs as a suspect?" suggested Harper.
"Yes, but when we have a murdered pensioner who was last seen speaking to this guy then it becomes a fecking major concern and everyone is a suspect."

Clara took this moment to add some more information,
"A female escort was arrested at the scene, and she claims to have had a prearranged 4pm appointment with a client who told her to undress in the bedroom. The bedroom was in the flat in which Ms Shaw lived. The young lady thought the location was strange and clearly not the bedroom of a man who was about to get married, but she didn't give it a second thought as,

*in her own words, **she has done some weird stuff since becoming a sex worker**."*

"Does she know who booked her?"
"She doesn't know him, but she described him as a male, 6 foot tall, wearing a blue hoodie and a baseball cap. He spoke with a strong Yorkshire accent and paid her £300 for one hour which is double what she would normally charge."
"Was this man picked up on any CCTV?" asked Dani.
"No. We only have her word that he ever existed."
"We all done?" asked Gallows. *"Is it ok if I carry on now."*
Clara nodded, *"Indeed, please continue."*

Exeter.

"Liam Warren Davis, 34-year-old male. Stabbed and then set alight in a side road not far from Exeter station. As far as we can tell he was of no fixed abode and has no immediate family. The page was found inside the wallet of a Mr Ashley Rigby who had reported his wallet stolen the previous day. There isn't much more to add to that. We have no footage of our attacker entering Exeter or of him leaving. So, there is no evidence to suggest it was Kane."
Gallows turned his attention to Dani.
"It's almost like someone else had been there. A stabbing that went wrong, body set alight. Not how our man usually operates is it?"

Everyone in the room knew exactly what Gallows

was insinuating, and Harper did not like it. The problem was, it made sense, but it can't be true. Harper cupped her head in her hands as Gallows continued.

Folkestone.

"Victim was named as Noah Fisher. A 29-year-old male who was attacked with a hammer in a public toilet. He was at Radnor Park with his girlfriend and her mother. He has no dependants, and his immediate family are all from Leicester. He moved down to Folkestone to be with his girlfriend about 8 months ago. This became the reason why I was asked to pick this up as Noah was the son of General Alexander Fisher. Top brass of the British armed forces and long-time associate of mine."
"Hang on, what? Why didn't I know anything about this?" asked Clara.
Gallows looked over toward her and tilted his head. Holding eye contact, he continued to talk.

Gloucester.

"Our next one is Steven Owens, 28 and our first black victim."
"Wait," interrupted Clara, *"What has that got to do with anything."*
"What?" Gallows asked innocently.
"Why is his skin colour relevant?"
"It's all relevant DCI Marsh as you will soon find out,

if you let me finish."

"Harper could you pass me the jug of water please." Clara poured herself a drink as Gallows continued.

"So, Steven Owens was killed with a direct cyanide injection into his lower back. There was a lot of confusion at the scene and took some time to determine the cause of death and question those in attendance. No one has been arrested for the murder. The Alphabet page was posted to the supermarket where the incident took place two days later and the post mark indicates that the letter was posted locally which means our killer stayed in Gloucester for at least one night after the attack."

"So did you check the hotels and places like that?" asked Harper.
Gallows chuckled, *"Ya really are yas Daddy's girl aren't ya."*
"Or maybe he lives in Gloucester?" replied Harper.
"Bingo!" Gallows pointed at Harper, *"This is what I believe is the case. We know he is from Southampton and has a property in the north of England but to cover the ground he has without detection suggests he has various locations across England."*

"We have already established this," said Clara, *"let's get on shall we and save the theories for later. I just want to deal with the facts right now."*

Hereford.

"A white male believed to be in his late thirties who was known locally as Dunny, was found stabbed to death in broad daylight on Gomond Street. Now this is interesting as no page was found at the scene or has been located since, but we believe strongly that this is the work of Kane."

"Why?" asked Dani.
"Ah it speaks! Thought we'd lost you there for a minute. The location of the stab wound was the same as previous kills and of a few that followed. The method was also the same, serrated edge down and the knife forced into the victim with the wound being made as big as possible so the victim would die from that one stab wound."

Everyone waited for Dani to respond.
"No, that's ye done, is it?" Gallows asked sarcastically.

Ipswich.

Barry 'Baz' Walker, a 26-year-old male from the Ipswich area was working on a social studies project on how the public reaction to the homeless differs from town to town, or something like that. It's safe to say he didn't complete this project as he was stabbed and then set alight, along with his tent and belongings. It took a while to identify him, but Kane managed to fill in the blanks for us as he sent a photo of a dying Mr Walker to the local nick. As with other correspondence he has sent, he marked the message with the letter I.

Jarrow.

"Kenny 'Dorset' Westerley, 20-year-old male who was beaten within an inch of his life and then dumped over the side of the station bridge into the path of an incoming metro train. Clara, would ye mind carrying this on for a wee moment."

Gallows excused himself and walked out of the room.

"Ok yep," Clara quickly fumbled around for her notes and continued.
"Although this attack happened during the day, and there were witnesses, and CCTV coverage on both platforms we have not been able to tag this to Kane until an alphabet page was found in the trouser pocket of our victim."

"What do you mean you couldn't tag this on Kane?" Dani interrupted, *"How useless are you."*

*"For your information Miss Palmore, we were able to identify Kane at the location but that was two hours or so before Kenny was killed. At the time of Kenny's death, we have clear footage of the attack and the attacker, but his face does not match any previous descriptions we have of Kane. We have a witness statement which confirms our killer stayed at the scene after the attack as someone saw **a man acting odd on a nearby bench**."*

Dani continued her questions, *"How can you act odd when sitting on a bench?"*

"Because" replied Clara, *"if someone gets crushed and decapitated at a train station people do not usually sit calmly and watch from a distance."*

Dani sat back into her chair.
"At the scene we uncovered the Alphabet page for J along with a poem which I shall read to you.

A boy can dream
even find grace
here in Jarrow

kill lee maccles

"In case you hadn't noticed the letter at the start of each word corresponds to the order in which the letters flow in the alphabet. A boy can dream even find grace here in jarrow, kill lee maccles."

At this point Dani chuckled.
"What Dani, what?" Clara asked firmly. *"What is so amusing."*
Dani apologised, *"I'm sorry, I just find this so stupid. He's telling you where he's going, Leeds, Macclesfield, and you still can't catch him."*

At that point Gallows walked back into the room. Clara stared at the tired looking old drunk and knew the only reason why he left the room was because he didn't want to look stupid having to admit that they really dropped the ball on this one.

"K?" said Gallows as he sat down.

Kidderminster.

"Ralph Bernard-Harris, 61-year-old male suffered a fatal stab wound to the neck. This was done whilst he was driving and resulted in a car crash which also injured two other people. The crash made it difficult at first for the onsite team to determine the cause of death, but it does tell us that our man was hiding in the car and attacked Mr Harris from behind like a fecking coward. There is no CCTV from the scene and no witnesses, but we have evidence that Kane was spotted in a supermarket car park where we believe he scouted his victim prior to the attack."

Leeds.

"Saskia Lloyd, 23-year-old female from Reading who was visiting friends. She was born in Leeds but moved to Reading to be with her boyfriend of four years. This was another attack where the body was set alight. Our teams were able to determine that Ms Lloyd was dead before the fire was started. Her clothes had been removed but no signs of any sexual assault."

Gallows turned away from the laptop.
"Was he a fecking pervert when ya were fucking him?"
"Brian," interrupted Clara, *"I don't think that's appropriate."*
"I've been told about the consent tattoo he wanted ye

to get. Was he a necro... whatever it's called?"
"Necrophiliac?" replied Dani. "He wasn't a practising necrophiliac, but everyone has fantasies."
"What the feck is wrong with ya girl."
Dani offered the slightest smile, *"So much."*

Brian put his hand in his pocket and pulled out a bottle of whiskey. Unscrewing the lid, he took a large gulp and continued.

Macclesfield.

"Kendall Bellows, 19-year-old male who was stabbed multiple times. Five to be precise. Once in each eye, each ear and again in the mouth. This final one was delivered with such force that his jaw was also broken but he was dead long before that had happened.
The page was handed to us after the known associates of Mr Bellows were questioned about the attack. One lad, Raj Gujral was given the page by the attacker who called himself the Black Vulture but for whatever reason. Mr Gujral was unable to identify the man who murdered his friend."

"Vulture?" asked Harper.
"Black vulture." replied Gallows.
"What does that mean?"
"You know what missy, we don't fecking know. We know it's our man but why he invented this nickname we have no idea."
"One question," said Dani raising her hand. *"If this Raj guy spoke to Kane, then why didn't he offer up a*

description? Why did you just say he was unable to identify him?"

Clara tilted her head, waiting for a response.

Gallows stood up. *"I think a natural break is needed right now, don't yas? Gin, keep an eye on her."*
Dani shook her head in disbelief.
"You need the toilet?" asked Gin.
"No." Dani replied.

The next ten minutes were the quietest Dani had experienced all day. She used this time to reflect on what has been said to her and the accusations she faced. She sat hunched over the table running her fingers through her short black hair when she heard Harper's voice.
"I got you a coffee."
Dani lifted her head. *"Thanks."*
"You, ok?"
"No, not really."
"Stop talking yas." said Gallows as he entered the room
"Fuck sake man." Dani sighed as Harper walked back to her seat.
"Is everyone back? Great, let's continue."

Newport.

"59-year-old Mary Newton was found drowned in a public toilet shortly after 8pm in Newport on the Isle of Wight. She had been stabbed in the neck and

suffered injuries to her head. The page was stuffed into her knickers which we assume was done after she had died. This is the first time Kane has left the mainland and if we're being honest, it wasn't a destination we had pegged."

"What do you mean, pegged." asked Harper.

"We were building a strategy around his movements and were expecting him to stay nearer to Macclesfield, but he didn't and, it threw us off the scent for a wee while."

Oxford.

"Sama Ebeid, a 30-year-old student was found dead at her flat. There is no CCTV coverage in the area, but we do have a witness, a Mr Newstead who saw a man lurking around the area shortly before Miss Ebeid entered the block. The page was found in the jacket pocket of Miss Ebeid which suggests, along with the autopsy reports, that she was attacked from behind and probably the moment she walked into her home."

"How many of these do you have?" asked Harper.

Portsmouth.

"Here our killer has obviously decided to kill twice in P and not visit the letter Q. Otis Jackson, a 58-year-old male was found dead in an abandoned retail unit. He was of no fixed abode. The page was found forced down his throat. Now this was the letter Q. The letter P was found pushed into the empty eye socket of a

Mr Thomas Clayton. His death was in a similar fashion to young Kendall, but this appears to be less controlled. Mr Clayton suffered multiple wounds to his face and neck."

"Multiple wounds?"
"Yes Clara. We have yet to determine the weapon used but it was not a knife even though the skin and skull had been penetrated by some type of bladed weapon. I also want to add that, at this point I believe Kane's masterplan is beginning to unravel."
"What makes you say that?" asked Dani.
"The unexpected jump off of the mainland to the Isle of Wight. The focus on ethnic minority groups in both Oxford and Portsmouth. He's panic killing."
Dani laughed. *"What the fuck is panic killing?"*
Gallows did not find this funny. *"He killed twice in Portsmouth. One of them being the letter Q. Why? Because we don't think he had planned to go this far into the alphabet, or he is losing his bottle. Either way this makes him really dangerous."*
"I'm sorry Brian," interrupted Clara. *"I'd say he has always been pretty bloody dangerous, wouldn't you agree?"*
"Yes I suppose, but he was contained within his own game. Who's to say he won't just lump all the remaining letters together and take out a school or shopping centre. Go on a shooting spree."

Dani was offended by the suggestion.
"No, that's not how his mind works. Yeah, it appears he's changed the rules of the game a little to suit him

and killed twice in Portsmouth but that doesn't mean he is in a state of panic."
"That's an interesting point of view. Have I touched a nerve there girl?"
"Brian, can we get this finished please." asked Clara.

Rochdale

"Summer Ryan was just 17 when she was pushed into oncoming traffic. The elderly driver of the first car to hit her died a few days after the incident, and three others were injured. No page was recovered at the scene, but a few days later an email was received with the subject heading R, which contained two photos of Miss Ryan. Both taken from behind her and both, we believe to have been taken just seconds before she was attacked. There is CCTV but as we've come to expect now, our attacker was masked so identification is tricky at best."

"So now what?" asked Dani.
"So now, what?" repeated Gallows, *"I'll tell you girl. You are going to be locked in a room with two local Bobbies who will keep an eye on you until three when we will meet again to go through the final bits before the appeal at five."*
Gallows grabbed his laptop and bag.
"The next few hours should give you enough time to understand what has been going on and to formulate some words that are going to appeal to yas ex.

With that Gallows and Gin left the room.

"How are you feeling?" Clara asked Dani.
"I need something to drink."
"Harper can you get a drink and some food for Dani please."

Harper nodded and left Clara and Dani alone.
"He's a massive cunt."
Clara smiled, *"Yes he is, but..."*
"No but, he's all cunt. How dare he talk to me the way he did, and everyone lets him get away with it."
"This is a game Dani, and we all have our role to play within it. Gallows likes to think he's the King but with the same power moves as the Queen, but he's a Bishop at best."
"I don't know what the fuck you are talking about."

Clara laughed, *"Chess. I guess you don't play."*
"Do I look like a fucking chess player?"
"No, I guess not. Dani, can you do me one favour."
"What?"
"Stop the fucking swearing."
Dani smiled, *"I'll do my best."*

"Excuse me ma'am we are going to have to ask you to leave as per Detective Galloways instruction."
A young PC was stood at the door, looking awkward having just told a senior officer to leave the room. At that same moment Harper appeared holding a couple of bottles of water and a sandwich.
"Sorry, you can't go in there."
"Why, who are you?"

"As per Detective Galloways instruction we have been..."
"Yes, yes ok whatever. Can you give this to Dani."

Harper handed over the lunch and waited by the door for Clara. Dani took the food and drink from the officer and opened the bottle of water.
"What do I do when I need a piss after I've drunk this lot."
Clara looked back, *"Behave."*
Dani smiled as the door was closed. *"Behave? Why start now."*

Outside the station it was quiet. A couple of journalists had caught wind of what was happening today and were parked up, trying to not look out of place. Hoping to steal a few photos of the participants in today's briefing.

"Look at them fecking idiots." said Gallows pointing at the car. *"Why do they think no one can see them?"*
"No idea Brian," replied Clara. *"Now, are you sure you know what you're doing?"*
"Yes of course. I know what that girl is up to. She got one over on Harper, but it won't wash with me. Dickie is on his way and will be at the briefing."
"Speaking?" asked Clara.
"No, no. I figure having him in attendance will put further pressure on Dani and she will slip up. Maybe not at the briefing itself but after. She will tell us where Kane is going to be and that's when we strike.

Dani believes everything we have said to her so far and if she does have contact with Kane, then now is when she will have to show her hand."

Clara inhaled deeply through her nose and closed her eyes.
"Ok Brian, yes. Let's carry on with this way of doing it."
"I was never after your permission." replied the Irishman.
"Now, I'm going to assign Gin to basically shadow Dani. Where she goes, he goes. It's not negotiable, it's happening."

Clara nodded hoping this unscheduled meeting would soon end.
"And one other thing. Look after Harper, she's a good girl."
"But won't Dickie be with her?"
"Me and Dickie have some business to attend to, so no."

Clara shrugged her shoulders. *"Alright, I'll keep her with me."*
"Great, I'll see yas this afternoon."

THE APPEAL

"Miss Palmore. Excuse me, Miss Palmore."
"Yes what? Oh, it's you. What do you want Gin?"
"This way please."

Dani was escorted out of the room and down the corridor of magnolia walls and crime inspired graphics focused on drink driving, domestic violence, and knife crime. Dani noticed that the knife crime posters were very specific in their intent. Not to raise awareness of the obvious danger that can be found on the streets, but to remind Dani that she was about to reveal the identity of the Alphabet Killer to the whole world.

"Have these posters been put up here on purpose?" she asked Gin.
"All the information has been posted on purpose. This is a police station."

Maybe he was right. Maybe he wasn't. Maybe he was just unaware, too stupid to realise the obvious mind games that are in play right now. The guy in the poster is wearing a dark hoodie, his face blurred out, and it was obvious to Dani who the poster was about.

As they reached the end of the corridor, Clara was there to greet them.

"How are you feeling?"
"Your mind games won't work on me," replied Dani. *"Did you put this poster here on purpose?"*
Clara nodded, *"Yes. Absolutely. What you're about to do is incredibly brave but also incredibly difficult. I have read into every angle on this case and for me it is as black and white as it looks. Kane is guilty of these crimes and sadly along the way you became controlled and manipulated."*

"So, I'm not getting arrested then?"
"What for?"
"Gallows is convinced..."
"Gallows is throwing his shit about and hoping some of it sticks. Richard sold Gallows the story that you came into their life and, basically, smashed everything up."
"Like a wrecking ball."
"Maybe? Or bowling ball?"

Dani chuckled, *"Either way I'm a big ball of destruction aimlessly smashing into stuff."*
"No, I don't believe you're aimless. Like a wrecking ball, or bowling ball..." It was at that moment Clara stopped and finished what she was going to say, in her own mind.

*"Like a wrecking ball, or bowling ball
you have a clear target in mind,
and you know that when you make contact,
something will collapse."*

Clara felt uneasy, perhaps she had underestimated Dani all along. Now was not the time to open that particular conversation, especially as Gallows was walking toward them.

"Yas ready then girl?" Dani did not acknowledge the question. *"I see ye going to be as cooperative as usual."*

The press room was a new experience for Dani. Seated behind a light brown wooden desk, between Clara and Gallows felt so uncomfortable, so unnatural. She had spent so much time in the company of them both yet right now, at this moment, she felt alone, vulnerable.

In front of the table stood five cameras. The faceless rectangles stared unblinking toward Dani. Red lights flickering acting as a reminder that they were ready to capture her every word.

There was nowhere to hide. A few people stood near the back of the room who didn't appear to have any purpose, plus a couple of junior officers.

As Dani continued to look around the room the door opened and in walked Harper.

Dani exhaled and smiled. Her shoulders dropping, tension easing, as she felt she finally had a friend in the room. Harper acknowledged Dani but did not smile.

"*Why isn't she smiling?*" Dani thought to herself. "*What have I done wrong now?*"
It was then her questions were answered. Richard was right behind her and once they were seated a lone voice from the back of the room began counting down.

"*Going live in five... four...*

Dani lowered her head and closed her eyes. The countdown had begun, and this was it. This was the moment the mask comes off and Kane is revealed. Wherever Kane is right now, she hoped he was watching, listening, and most importantly, paying attention. Dani took in a deep breath and opened her eyes.

DCI Marsh began the briefing.

"*Thank you to everyone for attending from all of the major news companies. Your support with this matter is much appreciated.*"

"*There is no one here,*" thought Dani. "*What is she talking about.*"

"*The Alphabet killer has been running rampant across the country for some time now and we, up to this point, have been unable to put a name to this individual, until today. We have very strong reason to believe the man we are looking for is Aiden Elliot, but also, is known as Kane Azika. As you can see by the images on the screens to my left, we have photo cap-*

tured him at each of the following destinations. Basingstoke, Cambridge, Doncaster, Folkestone, Gloucester, Hereford, Ipswich, Jarrow, Kidderminster, Leeds, Macclesfield, Oxford and Rochdale. We have yet to place him in Andover, Exeter, Newport or Portsmouth, but we can confirm that he was present at these locations as we found his calling card. We can confirm what we have dubbed, the calling card, are in the form of pages which appear to be from a child's alphabet book. Our research concludes that these pages are not from available anywhere in the UK, so please do not attempt to replicate these pages. I know there are numerous images and theories circulating online as well as a Kane Azika twitter page, which we are currently unable to verify its authenticity. We know Kane Azika has been using masks to commit a number of the dreadful attacks so that has prevented us from forming a strong photo ID of him, until now. As you can see from these images, again to my left, we now know exactly who he is. You will begin to see a stronger police presence on the streets of our towns and cities as we try to put a stop to this before he is able to complete his game. In the meantime, please be extra vigilant and report anything that can help our investigation. The number is up on the screen. I want to hand over to this young woman who has helped with our investigation, and she has a message for Aiden Elliot."

Clara took a step back as Dani moved from her seat and placed herself in front of the quiet yet invisible audience.

"Hello. Thank you. Erm, I want to reach out to you, Aiden. I want you to hand yourself in and end this attack on so many innocent people. Please listen, we are here to help. The Styx is calling the ferryman and now would be the right time to come home. Please Aiden, if you're watching this, come home. The Duke is lonely."

"Thank you," said Clara as she moved Dani away from the microphone. *"That is all we have time for right now and as I said, if you have any information, please contact the numbers that are appearing on your screens. Thank you."*

"What are you playing at?" Clara barked.
Dani looked confused, *"What am I playing at, what?"*
"Come home Aiden. What are you saying to him?" Clara turned her attention to the nearest person with a laptop. *"I want to see what she said. Play it back."*

"Hello. Thank you. Erm, I want to reach out to you, Aiden. I want you to hand yourself in and end this attack on so many innocent people. Please listen, we are here to help. The Styx is calling the ferryman and now would be the right time to come home. Please Aiden, if you're watching this, come home. The Duke is lonely."

Marsh played it back a couple more times and faced Dani. *"The Styx is calling? The Duke?"*
"Look, I had a moment of panic. I've never done this

before."
"Why did you say that to him?"
"I don't know!"
"It's the book, isn't it?" Harper joined the conversation. *"You were quoting from the book."*

Dani bit her top lip and wondered who was next to inject their opinions on what just happened. Gallows, where is Gallows?
"You clever little bitch."
Dani smirked, *"Ah there he is."*
"Ye played us all, eh! Pretending to be the victim when all along yas knew exactly what yas were doing. Well, it never washed with me. I knew ye were rotten the moment I first clapped eyes on ye."

Dani looked around the room. Does everyone now believe that she is a part of this? An accomplice to the Alphabet Killer? Dani closed her eyes to try and drown out the accusations, the anger, the projected frustrations but it was no good. There were too many voices, too much pressure. Something had to give…

YORK

Sixteen hours after the appeal and Dani is still at the station, locked up in a holding cell until she is willing to cooperate. The appeal certainly created some hysteria within the briefing room, and how much of that was felt by the public as the feed went live, who knows?

On the other side of the door there was banging, and muffled words could be heard. Dani stood up, and as she did the door opened.

"Are you willing to play ball yet Dani?" asked Clara.

"Where's Harper?" Dani replied.

"She's here, with Gin."

"And the two old men?"

"I assume you mean Gallows and Dickie, they left a few hours ago."

"You know those two are dodgy don't you."

Clara directed Dani out of the cell.

"Don't worry about them now. We need to get to the bottom of what happened yesterday."

Dani rolled her eyes in response.

"Don't be like that. Please, work with me on this," said Clara. *"It's turning into a bit of a farce, and I can do*

without the aggro from above."

A short walk reunited Dani with Harper, but it wasn't the positive reconciliation she had hoped it would be.
"Why are you giving me the cold shoulder Harp?"
"I don't know what I can say to you anymore. I'm trying so hard to be calm and this, this is about the best you're going to get out of me."
Dani slowly nodded her head, *"Yep, yep ok."* She looked at Harper, then over to Clara. *"You win. Ok, you win."*
"What do you mean?" asked Clara.

Dani sat down on the nearest chair.
"You win, I'll cooperate. I'll tell you what you need to know. He's going to be in York."
"I think we all know that." replied Harper.
"Harper please listen, I know where he lives. He has a property there and I'm going to be honest now, he is there. I know he's there and this is his address."

Dani passed Harper a scrap of paper on which Dani had scribbled an Address in York with a YO30 postcode.
"What is this?" asks Clara.
"An address in York where we will find Kane, apparently.

Clara takes the paper from Harper and instantly gets onto her phone.
"The property has been purchased under the name Jack Hyde."

"What!" Harper turns round, a look of absolute disgust on her face.
"Jack Hyde, as in Mr.Hyde. Jackal and Hyde?"
Dani couldn't help but correct her, *"It's Jekyll."*
Through gritted teeth Harper replied with a simple, *"Fuck you."*

Dani pushed herself off the chair and onto the floor.
"What name did you say was given?" asked Clara as we walked back into the room.
"Jack Hyde." mumbled Dani.

Clara continued her phone conversation as Harper knelt next to Dani. In a moment of controlled rage, she grabbed a hold of Dani's hair and pull her head back.
"Look at me you little bitch. You have been sitting on this and allowing the deaths of so many innocent people. These murders are as much on your head as they are his.
Dani didn't react.
"Well, what have you got to say for yourself."

Dani looked up with tired eyes.
"I have nothing to say. I'm tired, and I just want this to end.
"Oh, this will end because, I have had enough." replied Harper.
"I know, me too."
"No, I've had enough of this. You. I have enough of you and the constant lies."

"I haven't lied to you.
Harper couldn't believe what she had just heard.
"Are you for real! Everything about you is a lie."
"What does that mean? I haven't lied to you. I've kept information from you but that isn't lying."
"When is he going to be in York?"

Dani did not answer. Instead choosing to once again stare at the floor.
"WHEN IS HE GOING TO BE IN YORK?" Harper yelled.
"Now. He's there now."
"How do you know?"
"The Grand Old Duke. G.O.D. It's in the book."
"That fucking book. THAT MOTHERFUCKING BOOK!"
"Yes, the book. It's all there."

Harper didn't want to hear anymore.
"Gin, I've had enough. Keep this crazy bitch away from me."
Before leaving the room Harper stopped and faced Dani one last time.
"When this is all done & you've been locked up with that bag of shit bloke of yours, I'm selling the flat and I don't ever want to see you again."

Dani sat without expression as Harper walked away, *"When they were up, they were up. And we will go down, will go down."*
"What are you saying?" asked Gin.
"Nothing. I'm not feeling too good. Can I go to the

bathroom?" Gin didn't have time to answer as Clara was calling them.
"Get your shit together we are going to York. Gin, bring her."
"She wants to go to the bathroom…"
"Now! Bring her now, we don't have time for this."

Gin lifted Dani from the floor and escorted her out of the building and into the back of his car. From his position in the car park, he could see Clara driving off with Harper and another officer.
"I'm going to be sick Gino."
"My name is Gin and if you want to be sick do it out of the window. We do not have time to wait. They have already left."

The drive from Birmingham to York was expected to take more than two hours, but thanks to some well-placed road closures at critical junctions, Clara was able to get to YO30 in under 100 minutes.

"How did you learn to drive like that?" asked Harper as they exited the vehicle.
"When you've been in this game as long as I have, you pick up a few tricks here and there."

Clara turned to the officer that accompanied them.
"You stay here. I have a team of officers from York on their way and your job, until then, is to prevent anyone from entering or leaving the building."
"Leaving. How do I do that?"
"You serious?" replied Clara. *"This area is a crime*

scene. We have a potential serial killer upstairs and you're worried about how to stop people leaving. Liaise with the other officers when they arrive."
"But..."
"No but! No one enters and no one leaves. Simple!"
"Shouldn't we wait outside for Dani and Gin?" asked Harper.
"Probably but I want to nail this bastard now. We've wasted enough time already. I have instructed Gin to call me as soon as they arrive. They shouldn't be too far behind us."

Via the stairwell they made their way up to the third floor, and they focused their attentions on flat number nine.

"Stop," whispered Clara as they approached the door. *"It's open."*
"What do we do?" asked Harper.
"Stay behind me."
Clara slowly pushed the door open and quietly entered, but the silence was broken as Clara let out an exasperated, ***"Fuck!"***

The flat was empty
No furniture.
No furnishings.
No electrical goods, nothing.

"It's empty. The place is empty!"
At that moment Clara knew that the alphabet game they were playing was bigger than her. Bigger than Dickie, Gallows, all of them. Was this all

the work of Kane, or Dani?
"The place is empty Harper. We've been had."
"Like in the Frank Hunt story."
"The book?"
Harper nodded, *"Yeah, but in this one there were three items left in the property. Check the rooms to see if anything has been left."*
Clara made her way to the bedroom and Harper moved along the corridor to the bathroom, and there it was. Sat on top of the closed toilet seat was a blue envelope.
The same size as a birthday card, but this card let off a pretty bad smell.
For a moment Harper was confused, maybe someone had taken a shit and not flushed it, but then it dawned on her. She picked up the envelope and sure enough there was what felt like a card inside.
"This is Dude Ray. Shit! This is one of those cards."
Harper held her breath and pulled open the envelope. As she did the smell got worse, aided by the fact there were no other smells to counter it, Harper felt sick.
She pulled out the card. On the front, in big colourful letters was a riddle.

**If womb is pronounced *woom*, and
tomb is pronounced *toom*,
then shouldn't bomb be pronounced... BOOM?**

Harper frowned, *"That doesn't make any sense."*
Opening the card, she was met with the following

message.

Dearest human, If you have found this card then it is because I am dead. This isn't a suicide note nor is it a written confession, it exists to let you know that you are going to be number twenty-five and twenty-six. Thank you for playing along and I hope to see you in Hell. All my love, Kane.

Even though the message on the front of the card made no sense, what was written inside did. Was this it? Was this the moment that she became nothing more than a number in a sequence. A name in a story told years later to kids who have a sick, morbid fascination with serial killers.

Harper heard a noise, and she felt her blood run cold. So this is what fear feels like? Was it him? Had she just been set up by Dani and sent to her death?
"You, ok?" asked Clara.
"I don't think we're safe here." replied Harper as she handed the card over. *"We have to leave."*
Clara opened and read the card.
"What is this and why does it smell so bad."
Harper didn't reply.

As Clara was about to ask Harper a second time her phone rang. It was Gin.
"I'm sorry but she's gone."
"What, what do you mean."
"Dani. She went to the bathroom and never came back out."

"What is it you are telling me exactly."
"She's gone. Vanished."

Clara pulled the phone away from her head and screamed.
A couple of deep breaths later and she was ready to continue the conversation.
"Talk me through what happened."
"I told you she said she needed to go to the bathroom. Well, she vomited in my car. She vomited everywhere. I took her to the services and escorted her to the bathroom. I waited and waited and then asked a lady who came out of the bathroom if she had seen anyone else in there, she said no, so, I went in. All the cubicles were empty. She was gone."
"Did she climb out of a window?"
"There are no windows."

Clara was silenced by the revelation.
"Gin, get back to Birmingham now."

Clara ended the phone call and ran outside to where Harper was sat on the kerb.
"Dani has disappeared."
Harper looked up at Clara, *"What?"*
"She pulled a fast one on Gin and now she has gone."
"I don't understand. Gin is better than that."
"Whatever she did, it worked and now she has vanished."
"Where were they?"
"I didn't ask but I would imagine not too far away. Somewhere between here and Leeds I guess?"

"Leeds?"
"I'll call Gin and see where they were when she ran."

Harper held her head in her hands, and she stared at the dead beetle that lay next to her left foot. In an attempt to process what had happened, she began to think out loud.

How did she know he was in York?
Was he ever in York?
What was the point in all this?
Why tell us where Kane is, who he is and then just run away.
Why me?
FUCK!!!

"Harper, I have spoken to Gin." Clara appeared breathless; Harper assumed this was down to stress rather than her running anywhere. *"What did he say?"*
"They were at the Ferrybridge services which is about a 40-minute drive away from here. I've told Gin to go back and get as much information as he can and check all CCTV so we can build a picture and understand what exactly happened."
"How long is that going to take?"
"I don't know. Let me get bomb squad down here and..."
"Bomb squad. What?"
"We have to be careful. That message on the card, bomb, boom. I think we were supposed to be walking into a trap."

Harper stood up and held Clara's arm. *"You ok?"*
"No." Clara replied bluntly. *"No, I'm not. How did this get so out of hand? We had everything in place, ready to attack and now we have no Kane and no Dani. What has happened?"*
"I don't know." replied Harper.
"Shit," said Clara as her phone began to ring. *"It's Gallows."*

Clara took a deep breath and answered.
"Brian, what do you know?"
There was no reply.
"Brian, are you there?"
"Oh sorry yas, to be sure to be sure. Feck all of the potatoes and feck a leprechaun."
Clara removed the phone from her ear and put it on loudspeaker.

"Sorry Brian I didn't quite catch that. What did you say?"
"Hi Clara," said a familiar voice. *"I'm sorry but Brian can't come to the phone right now."*
Harper grabbed the phone. *"Dani? What…"*
"What, what?" replied Dani. *"Or should that be wat, wat!"*
"That's a terrible Irish accent Dani," said Clara *"Is Brian with you?"*
"No, he's somewhat incapacitated right now. I knew I'd get away from Gin. The guy has seen my tits. Any bloke who has seen a woman's tits is immediately owned."
"You knew he was there back at the hotel room. That's

why it took you so long to cover up." said Harper.

"Ah, I'm on loudspeaker am I. Well listen up. I am tired of you all thinking I have something to do with this whole Kane bullshit. All I ever did was open up and let you know that I knew who the killer was. I showed you the book. I did everything I could to make this all stop, yet you kept throwing it back in my face. Accusing me of being a part of this. Think about it. How is it even possible?"

Clara turned off the speaker and put the phone back to her ear.
"You listen to me Dani. I don't know where you are right now but if you make your way back to Birmingham we can sit, talk, and come to an agreement. I believe you still know more than you are telling us but I'm willing to forget that if you just help us track down Kane."

"Did the room go boom."

Clara looked at Harper and then realised what had happened.
"You love Harper deeply, don't you?"
"What makes you say that." replied Dani
"I think the flat was a trap and supposed to kill us. A bomb was going to detonate somewhere at some point, but it didn't. Kane was never there but set this explosive up to kill myself and Harper, make us numbers twenty-five and twenty-six, but you couldn't let that happen. You felt a surge of guilt, maybe? A way that this would somehow prove to Harper that you

never meant to hurt her and all along you had her…"
"Shut up or I hang up."
Dani's interruption signalled to Clara that she had struck a nerve.
"What's wrong Dani. Am I getting too close to the truth? Are you worried I'm going to expose your true identity."
There was no reply.

"Dani, don't play games. Answer me."
"Hello."
"Dani, stop pissing about."
"Hello?"
Clara realised that the voice on the other end of the phone was that of a child.
"Hello, who is this?"
"I'm Harvey. Who are you?"
With that Clara ended the call.
"What?" asked Harper.
"She's gone. Gave the phone to some kid and disappeared."
"What do we do now?"

Clara looked to sky for inspiration, *"I don't know. I honestly don't know."*

Basingstoke train station.

A single woman stood alone on platform two, not moving. Waiting, patiently.

On the opposite platform, a train pulled into the station and all the usual movement occurred. People getting on, people getting off. Each one of them with a plan for where they were going next. As the train slowly pulled away, the woman remained in place. As the crowds faded she saw who she had been waiting for.

A man, dressed in an identical way to her, baseball cap, sunglasses, grey jacket, and black jeans. It was like looking into a mirror.

Through the tinted windows of the glasses their eyes locked.

It was then, that Dani smiled. She knew everything had come together. As she stepped forward, a station announcement rang out.

> *The train now approaching platform*
> *2 does not stop at this station.*
> *Please stand clear of the platform edge.*

PORTRAIT OF THEM

by Daemon April

Dearest A

You slip and slide.
Grind, and thrust, and hold your breath.
Squeeze your eyelids tight, but it doesn't matter.
You'll shoot your load soon enough.
Am I ready? No, but that hasn't stopped you before.
Through gritted teeth you hide the shame.

Aiden, remember that the art of conversation is dead. No one speaks anymore and no one cares.
Aiden, remember when you were a child and that man abused you, over, and over again.
He beat you into the ground and stomped out your soul. Destroyed whatever innocence you had left.
The babysitter played games with you as she tested your sexual boundaries.

Aiden, remember that the art of conversation is dead. Actions speak louder than words.
Aiden, remember that violence speaks louder.
Every action you commit must be loud, disruptive and without regret. Centre your hatred, anger and revenge in the right way.
And remember, the right way is the only way. My way, is the right way.

We slip and slide.
Grind, and thrust, you hold your breath.
Squeeze your eyelids tight, but it doesn't matter.
You'll shoot your load soon enough.
Am I ready? Yes, and I never want you to stop.

Through gritted teeth, we are the same.

Aiden, remember when we made love. Every time was supposed to be the last time, yet somehow, always felt like the first time.
Aiden, remember when you were let down by the very people placed on earth to protect you.
I never let you down. I never did, and I never will. I will never let you die. Others tried so hard to make it happen, tried so hard to kill you. Remove you, destroy you.

All I ever wanted to do is to love you.
Aiden, remember that.
Read this and remember.
With your actions and my words, nothing will stand in our way.
Hold this near to your heart and your mind will make the right decisions.

Aiden, remember the words.
My words.

Zangara

I was twelve and he was twelve.
I had dark brown hair and he had black hair.
I'm now twenty eight, and he is still twelve.
His father, who was a big, physical brute of a man, walked into his bedroom one night, placed a pillow over his face and held it there until he stopped moving.
His father then went to the bathroom where his wife was showering and brutally stabbed her to death.
His father then went out into the garage and shot himself in the face.

I miss my friend.

When I was fourteen my father took a new job which meant we had to move 150 miles from Nottingham to Southampton. My father worked at the docks. I don't know what he did, but he worked long hours. He would come home, drink then sleep. Come home, drink then sleep. Come home, drink then sleep. Adult life seems shit to me.

When I was fifteen, I ran away from home. After twelve days I came back. I was loved and my parents promised to change whatever had made me run as long as I promised never to run again.

By the age of Seventeen I had run away from home three more times, and this time, was the last time.

I made a new friend.
He had no hair but lots of tattoos.

With my new friend I also got a new job, selling drugs to kids. It was easy.
Every day at kicking out time I would hang around a particular school and eventually I would spot that one kid. The one that's a little bit feral, a bit of a lost cause, and I would straight up offer him drugs. It rarely worked and when I got a *'no'* I moved onto the next school.
It never took long for me to get a *'yes'* rather than a *'no'* and once I was in, I was sorted.

I remember one school in particular; I befriended a kid called Mitchell and his mum was proper rough. Saying that, she was kind of attractive though, but attractive in the same way a wheelie bin would be attractive if you put a wig on it, covered it in make-up and gave it big tits. I say *'it'* because that's what she is, an *'it'*. With an IQ lower than my shoe size, she/it is always going to produce offspring that are an easy target for people like me.
I manipulate. I create unrealistic expectations that will often be dreamt about but never achieved. I promise happiness because money becomes very easy. People become dependent on my product and these retarded, fatherless children will be the next generation of dealers or smackheads. Either way, I win.

Prostitution was always going to be the next step.

Once I nailed the drugs it was time to move on, to bigger and better things.

The money made from these cum dumpsters was incredible.

An average day would bring in around £300 and that's just on one woman.

In less than five weeks of starting this I had eight women working for me, and with proper hygiene, and marketing, I managed to scrape around £40k a month, once I'd let the skanks have a bit of cash for their efforts.

FORTY THOUSAND A MONTH, sounds outrageous doesn't it, and it is. £40,000 a month is a potential half million over the course of a year.

Give or take a few thousand here and there depending on which of my staff survive the year or not.

In under a year, I had managed to accumulate £148,383 in savings. The rest I pissed against the wall, remember I am still a teenager.

A teenager with at least thirty years of life experience behind him.

A teenager that had no desire to live beyond the age of twelve.

A teenager that has just one emotion and that emotion is hate.

When I returned home at the age of nineteen, I saw before me two very elderly looking and disappointed people.

One used to be called mum, and the other used to

be called dad.
Now, they are just Helen and Daniel.

Helen and Daniel RIP.
I stood at their graveside.
At the age of twenty-one I should not be burying both parents at the same time, yet here we are.
I watched as they lowered the caskets into the ground, one on top of the other.
I suggested Daniel went in first with Helen on top as they were now bound together for eternity, Daniel would prefer that.

Strange to be at a funeral when it's both your parents getting buried, especially as I was in attendance on the day they both died. I didn't pull the trigger, but I did watch. I didn't defend them, but I did smile.

"Please" they kept saying, "Please don't do this."

Please. PLEASE.
It's a shitty little word. A password for the weak.

Por favor
Palun
Va rog
os gwelwch yn dda

Same word no matter how you say it.

Well Helen and Daniel said it over and over again. Until the trigger was pulled. Five bullets were fired in total. Two into the woman and three into the

man.
All shots above the neck, all shots were fatal.

I think back to the time when I was twelve.
He was also twelve.
My friend Kane Zangara will no longer breathe but he will forever live through me.

A family wiped away so quickly, without reason. Without an explanation as to why I lost my friend. My childhood. My parents.

RIP Kane. I will be with you again soon.

Martha and Gavin

"I don't think this storm is going to let up any time soon."
"Come away from the window Gavin, you're not missing anything."
"But I know my one true love will visit me tonight."
"What, in this weather? I doubt it very much."
"Has Nettle got everything ready just in case?"
"Yes, yes. It's all sorted. Same as it was yesterday, and the day before that."
"I hope she comes tonight. I will love her you know."
"Yes, but she needs to pass the test first. Only the most delicate will win the hand of my child."
"Oh, mother I am so excited. La la la, boo lumbar, I call Cupid."
"Please stop singing that stupid song.
"Sorry mother. I'm just so full of pretty gay butterflies."
"Hmmm, come and sit down and you can have some warm milk."
"Oh yummy."

❖ ❖ ❖

"Did you hear that?"
"Hear what?"
"There is someone at the door."
"Don't be foolish boy. Who would be out in this terrible

storm?"
"My love!"
"No Gavin, don't open the door. Oh great, too late."

"Hello, sorry to interrupt you but it's frightful out here and my horse was struck by lightning, so I've been travelling on foot for the past hour or so. Could I please get lodgings for the night?"

"Mother? Can she?"
"Of course. I'll ask Nettle to get everything ready."

"Please girl come in. What is your name?"
"Martha. Nice to meet you."
"I'm Gavin. Gavin Prince, nice to meet you too."
"Hi Gavin, is it possible I can get some dry clothes?"
"Oh yes of course. I think mother is getting that sorted for you."

"Ok thanks. This is a nice home you have."
"It belongs to father. He is away at the moment, overseas. I don't see so much of him, but I know he loves me. Mother tells me all the time."
"Where is your mother?"
"She will be here soon don't you worry."

"I really need to change my clothes that's all."
"You can take them off here if you want to? I can get you a towel. We have ever such fluffy ones."
"No, I'll wait."
"La la la, boo lumbar, I call Cupid. Do you believe in Cupid?"
"What do you mean?"

"Cupid. The son of Mars and Venus. Mars is the God of War and Venus the Goddess of Love. In turn Cupid and Psyche had a child called Voluptas."
"Right. You know your stuff."
"Roman mythology. Do you want me to show you my..."
"Sorry is your mother going to be long, I'm really not comfortable right now."
"Your clothes?"

"Yeah, and other things."

"Sorry for the delay young, sorry I don't know our name."
"It's Martha."
"I can answer for myself thank you."
"Sorry."
"Yes, I'm Martha Cess. Do you have some clothes I can change into?"
"A pleasure to meet you, Martha. Yes, Nettle has everything arranged for you in the guest bedroom. She is waiting for you at the bottom of the stairwell."
"Thank you, and wonderful to meet you both."

❖ ❖ ❖

"Why are you grinning like that Gavin?"
"Mother, I believe she is the one. I told you my love would visit me today and, oh shudder! She is Martha Cess. I am Gavin Prince. Prince Cess. Princess. She is my beautiful princess."

"She is beautiful, yes, but is she delicate enough for you?"
"I think she will be mother. I just know it. La la la, boo lumbar, I call Cupid."
"Calm down. The morning will tell us if wedding bells are on the horizon."
"Oh, mother I could skip across hot, melting tombstones."

"Excue me Ma Prince."
"What is it Nettles?"
"Ee the lady. He not happy in the get room."
"What's wrong? The clothes, the temperature of the room?"
"No ee bed. He not happy with bed."

"What's wrong mother?"
"Nothing. You stay here Gavin, and I will go and see what the problem is."

"Hello Martha, what's the problem?"
"I don't wish to sound ungrateful; I mean the change of clothes and your hospitality has been lovely but what is this?"
"It's your bed dear."
"Why so many mattresses? How is that even safe. If I manage to climb to the top, any movement and the whole thing will collapse. Is there a chance I could have a regular bed with the regular number of mattresses? One."
"To be honest with you Martha we have had many a

guest stay and no one has ever complained. It's the very best bed in the house."

"Really?"

"Indeed. Climb the ladder and you will see. It will be the best sleep you will ever have."

"Again, I don't wish to sound ungrateful..."

"Then shut up and climb the ladder."

"I'm sorry, did you just tell me to shut up?"

"It's been a difficult day dear. I do apologise."

"No, no, no. There is something going on here."

"Please. I'll go and make you some warm milk and once you've had a sleep, we can discuss it in the morning."

"Fuck your warm milk and I am not sleeping on that."

"I beg your pardon?"

"Do you think this is normal? Asking me to sleep on a bed some 12 feet above the ground. It's not stable. I could push this now and the whole thing would collapse."

"I'm sorry. Yes, you are right. I shall speak to Nettles and ask her to strip this down and make a regular bed for you."

"Thank you. Like I said I don't want to appear ungrateful and your kindness is heart-warming but, this is a bit weird, don't you think?"

"It's ok. I shall get Nettles to sort it out. NETTLES!"

"That's another thing. What's wrong with her? I don't understand what she is saying."

"We confiscated the letter S from her vocabulary."

"I don't even understand what that means."

"Ye Ma Prince."

"Kill our guest and put her in the garden with the others."

"Ye of core. Come with me plea girl, I will cut your throat."

"You kidding me? What are you talking about. Get your hands off me!"

❖ ❖ ❖

"Everything ok mother?"
"Yes Gavin, everything is ok."
"Is Martha resting."
"Yes darling. Like the others, she is resting."
"Outside?"
"Yes outside, with God. He will give her shelter for the night."
"I loved her."
"I know darling, but she just wasn't delicate enough for you."
"Can I see her?"
"Later yes."
"Can I play with her like I played with the others."
"Gavin you can do whatever you like with her once she is outside. I noticed you were having fun with Diana the other morning."
"I didn't know which hole to put my pee pee in so I went in her eye hole. It was so soft from the rain."

"You do make me laugh son."
"Mother, can I have some more warm milk?"
"Not right now. My nipples are still a little sore from earlier. Once we get Martha down to rest, I'll let you have a little bit before sleep. Does that sound good?"

"Yes, I suppose so. I'm going to go and look at the storm some more. Maybe my love will arrive soon."

MR DUDE RAY

Augustus Gordon Hayhurst never really liked his name, but on this particular morning, there were bigger things to worry about.
On his doormat lay 5 brightly coloured envelopes. One pink, two yellow and two baby blue. It wasn't his birthday, that was a couple of months back, and he wasn't celebrating anything; he lives alone with no spouse or dependants. Instead, today was the annual celebration of a certain **Mr Dude Ray**, an internet sensation. Well, maybe sensation is the wrong word to use but he was the creator of something we've all come to know now as Murder Day.

It started off with the first event taking place on November 18, 2006, in which, during a live stream **Mr Dude Ray** killed a spider. Doesn't sound like much but every kill must start somewhere.

In 2007 he went live and killed again. This time a wild, grey mouse. His method of killing wasn't anything creative or particularly enjoyable, he released the tiny critter from the humane trap, and stamped on it.

2008 was a budgie, followed in 2009 by a pigeon and in 2010 a kitten. The internet was made for cats and the moment he stamped on the head of that mewing tabby kitty, the world took notice.
For a whole year people speculated about what they had just watched and when the old video clips

were found, **Mr Dude Ray** became something of an invisible celebrity.

Unfortunately, November 18, 2011, took too long to come around and by the time it did, **Mr Dude Ray** was pretty much forgotten. Undeterred, **Mr Dude Ray** (let's call him **MDR** from now) went ahead and killed a rabbit. Held it up by the ears, put a blade into its mouth and pushed down as hard as he could, tearing the mammal in two.

The following year a squirrel was sacrificed live and the following year, a dog. A young black Labrador Retriever that was so happy to play when **MDR** walked into the room, but soon realised something was wrong. As the tail of the animal dropped between her back legs, **MDR** sat beside the quivering bitch and force fed it a lit firework.
He lit, then pushed the rocket deep down into her throat and clamped her jaw shut.
He sat beside her, and felt the BANG as the rocket exploded, but with nowhere to go. The dog was afraid but a lot smaller than **MDR** so had no chance of escaping, no matter how hard she tried. **MDR** kept the animals jaw clamped shut and waited for her to calm down. It didn't happen. In fact, nothing happened. The firework went out. He reached for another when the dog turned and bit him.

"Oh, you silly bitch." he shouted.
Grabbing the dog by the neck, he pinned her down and felt for the ribs. Once he found the thin bony

middle of the dog, he lifted his clenched fist and drove it as hard as he could into the helpless mutt.
Once.
Twice.
Three times was plenty.
The dog stopped moving and MDR sat still, staring at the camera. This went on for three minutes followed by a gradual fade to black.

After the fiasco that was the dog video, **MDR** properly prepared himself this time. As the video began, the first thing those sick souls who were watching got to see was a pig. Tied down in what looked like an empty shipping container, **MDR**, dressed in a large white coat and oversized plastic goggles, walked into shot and stood next to the pinned animal. Pulling out a stun gun of sorts, he rested the barrel on the top of the animal's head and signalled to a second person who was off camera to pass him something.

A hand clad in a yellow latex glove handed MDR a sandwich (the internet decided that it was a bacon sandwich but it was never confirmed), and after he took a large bite from it, he threw the remaining food at the pig then shot it right between the eyes. The animal lay motionless as a second gun was passed across the screen. **MDR** pressed It hard into the eye socket of the dead animal and shot a second time. Bending over he picked up a part of the sandwich from the floor and pushed it into the freshly expanded eye hole.

MDR finally got to that day when he killed his first human, and it was broadcast live for all to see. He recorded it all on camcorder and it wasn't a great viewing spectacle, it was very shaky, and the sound was horrible. It was filmed in a public toilet, so every time the knife was forced into the neck of the tramp, he would let out a tortured wail, and the sound would bounce around the ceramic shit house and into the very veins of **MDR**. He felt a surge of power, like the tramps very soul was being injected into him. This felt good. So good.

A lot of people got to see the video and was quickly labelled as being fake, I mean, who would do that and then post it online? Well, HE did.

The following year he did it again, and again the year after that.
Now he was internet famous and every year he did not disappoint.
Every death got more and more intense as the kills became more and more extreme and diverse. He killed with a hammer, he killed by throwing someone from a balcony. He even used cyanide on one occasion, but being the entertainer that he is, he saved the best for last.

In 2026, **MDR** went live with an estimated 66 million people watching. He was stood at the centre of a bridge, some 620m above the ground, staring into the camera. Now and then he would wobble which allowed the viewers to catch a glimpse of

the concrete far below him.
He held the camera up to his face and shouted;
I have carried the souls of my victims and now the final soul to be consumed will be my own.
Embrace me as I fall into the Styx where I shall be carried home by the Ferryman. This is my return to Zion!

And with that he fell.

His body was recovered a few hours later where he was pronounced dead at the scene.
As a tribute to **Mr Dude Ray**, Murder Day was created and on this most special of days it became customary to send people vile, abusive, and threatening letters or cards.

Augustus Gordon Hayhurst (August to his friends) looked down at his doormat and wondered why this year he got 5 cards. He always got one from his mother, but the other 4 were a mystery.
One thing to remember with Murder Day cards is that these are designed to offend and create mental tension.
Fun side note: a company by the name of **RotAromA** produced a new line of Murder Cards that were not only keeping with the tradition of being offensive but also came in 6 different odour options.

1. **Uranus Egg**
2. **Corpse Lily**
3. **Festival Toilet**
4. **Warm Sewage**

5.   **Anal Gland Discharge**
6.   **Tramp Vomit**

Would you consider the sending and receiving of greetings card a hate crime? Well, the capital of this once great nation registers approximately 50 hate crimes on an average day, yet on Murder Day this number increases tenfold.

August is weak. The cards waiting and festering on his doormat scare him.
After a few minutes he realises that he can't spend the whole day just staring at the envelopes. Walking slowly over to the cards, he crouches down.
They stink. At a guess, anal gland discharge?
As August continues to squat over his Murder Day offerings, he hears something he didn't want to be hearing right now.

Knock, knock, knock.
August froze with fear. The door is knocked again, this time louder.
It's 8:43am, the day has only just begun.

The Tale of Lola the Dog

Dale Stone was, and *was* is a very important word here, a respectable member of the community. Respectable in that he was a regular at the local church, had a part time job as a caretaker in the nearby school and still lived at home with his mother and sister. He was quiet, non-intrusive and always first to volunteer for any local events. He also killed small animals on a regular basis.

Dale Stone is a sick motherfucker and deserved everything he had coming to him. Sadly, it isn't much as the maximum jail term he will likely serve is five years. He is thirty-one now so still plenty of life left for him to enjoy once he has served his time.

It's true that he won't have a job to return to once he is released, and I can't imagine the church will be particularly welcoming once he returns, but you never know. The church has been known to forgive worse.

Let us back track a little to sixteen months ago. No, that's no good. That's when he was arrested. Let's go back twenty-two months to when he killed a hamster.

An innocent, ginger haired hamster.

No, no. Let's go back further. Let's go back forty-one months from today. That's round about the time he had sex with his sister. Full penetrative, non-consensual sex that lasted almost two minutes. This wasn't the first time he'd had an illegal sexual encounter. Some years prior to this, he gave his virginity to a chocolate brown Labrador retriever called Lola.

Lola was the family pet and Dale Stone was very close to the animal. Very, very close. They would spend a lot of time together and one thing he learned was that if he poured meaty gravy over his genitals and arse crack then Lola would happily lick him clean. After this revelation he became quite experimental.

He would pour gravy along with small chunks of meat all over his naked body and let Lola go to work. If he starved the animal for 24 hours then he was guaranteed a rampant licking. He even stuffed dog food up his arse once and when Lola licked the chunks from his anus, he ejaculated so hard he thought his head was going to explode. But the best was yet to come.

Using the starving technique, he waited for 36 hours before he fed Lola and after the obligatory meaty gravy arse rimming, he put the remainder of the meat in her bowl.

Lola was so hungry that she didn't pay much attention to what was going on behind her. Dale Stone who by this point was suitably aroused, was about to mount her.

Once inside his faithful hound he felt alive.

After this moment of passionate rape, Lola

got pregnant and after three months gave birth to five mutant huppies. Of those born, only one survived and it was quite unique. Its saggy skin was the colour of sewage diluted pink lemonade and it had patches of damp beige hair in the most random of places. It had two short stumpy arms but only one hand. The back legs were perfectly formed, if by perfectly formed you mean they looked like a couple of boomerangs inserted violently into the eye sockets of a dead bloated bullfrog.

Dale spent four days caring for this creature he had co-created before he decided to get rid of it, and to do that all he needed was a bath full of water, a hessian sack, a strong arm and some loud music.

Once the bath was ready, he picked up the pathetic looking creature and dropped it into the sack. He did consider stunning the animal first but liked the idea of watching it fight for life. He had control. All the control. This was making Dale feel aroused and he loved it.

With the Huppie in the bag he turned to his 80's style boombox and pressed play.

When will I, will I be famous. Were the words that filled the room as Luke and Matt Goss (and the other one) pushed their non-offensive 1980s pop onto the world with the album, PUSH.

As the music began, Dale held the sack under the water and once it realised what was happening the

Huppie began to kick, scream and fight for its life, but it was pointless.

As the song faded so did the life of this abomination.

That night, Dale and Lola fed off of the carcass of their child.

Lola remained a part of Dales life for a further 16 months.

Dale decided it would be best to bury her in the garden, problem was, Dale was physically weak and the hole he created wasn't deep enough to bury the whole dog, so Dale did what any good animal abuser would do, he chopped the beast up into chunks. Most of it was then buried in the hole and what remained, was shared throughout the week as the meat that accommodated the vegetables.

Domino Cortez. She/Her. They/Them. Shot/Dead.

On the 26th day of September 1991, Luisa Cortez gave birth to her fifth child. Yes, her fifth child but this was her first daughter. Four sons prior to this was great, they were all healthy and happy but Luisa wanted a daughter.

If truth be told, this baby girl who had been born into the Cortez family was the first conceived without the help of Oscar Cortez, the husband of Luisa. Instead, she fucked the young guy who worked at the bakery. He was seventeen years her junior and every time she saw him, she caught him staring at her big tits.

To be fair he apologised every time but the attraction was there. He wanted to know what was hiding beneath her clothing. He had an idea but wanted to see for himself the beauty of her mature body. He didn't care about stretch marks, veins or those saggy bits, he wanted to taste every last inch of her.

Luisa knew this and for eight months did her best to ignore his cravings but, we are all human and in the end she gave in. It wasn't a romantic story, but let's be honest, romance never really factors into it. A man shooting his sperm into an open vagina is the same no matter how fluffy you make the story. A fuck is a fuck. Paint it as pretty as you want it doesn't matter. It ends with some guy ejaculating in or on someone and that's it. Job done.

It took no more than twelve encounters for Luisa and her new, younger lover to realise that they were in love, but they could not be in love. Yes, this is another one of those stories where someone fucks someone else and what started off as a bit of fun turned into an obsession. He loved her voluptuous body, and she loved his young, firm cock. He celebrated every moment with as she did with him.
Back at home she was just a mother and a wife. Four boys and one husband. The same routine day after day. It became a chore, but she was made to feel grateful for what she had.

Four months after fucking her young lover for what became the final time, Luisa realised she was pregnant.
The reason it was the final time? The bakery closed down and she never saw him again.

Later that year, on the 26th day of September 1991, Luisa gave birth to her fifth child. A girl, she named Domino.

Domino was never accepted into the family as Luisa could not convince her husband that this child as his. He knew Luisa had a lover but at the time he didn't care. As long as he and his boys were looked after he didn't care what his wife got up to. He wasn't happy to welcome Domino into the world and yes, he was a fat, lazy bastard who fell out of love with his wife some years ago, but apparently still had feelings. Still had an emotional connection to reality even though he hid it so very well.

On the 19th day of January 1995, Luisa died. The circumstances surrounding her death were more than a little suspicious but an investigation was never launched as her body was never found. That's the great thing about a lazy police force, don't report a missing person and they won't ever investigate.

Life became very difficult for Domino after her mother died. Dominated at home by four older brothers and a father that never wanted her. It was almost a year to the day when the Cortez family said goodbye to Luisa that the abuse began.

At first it was considered mild bullying and name calling but it soon escalated into something much worse.
By the age of thirteen, Domino suffered her first miscarriage. Two weeks before her seventeenth birthday, she'd had her third.
On the 29th of September she celebrated her 18th birthday. She would have celebrated it three days earlier except she was in hospital, undergoing treatment for a broken jaw.
At least that is what she remembers.

As the new year bells chimed to welcome in the

start of a new decade, Domino realised that life was never going to improve if she stayed here with her abusive brothers. She had one more degrading thing to do before she could finally say goodbye and that was to get a gun.

Bruno Santiago was the local dealer and had his many fingers in many pies. I say many fingers as he was born with an extra pinkie on each hand, and that's not the weird thing about him.

Some say he was born without knees or elbows and at the age of 2 had his super straight legs and arms broken to allow for medical knees and elbows to be inserted.

This happened every 10 months until he reached the age of 16 when he was unable to receive any treatment which resulted in him remaining shorter than most and heavily scarred across the arms and legs.

Others say his mother gave birth to him as she was fleeing a gang attack. As she did so she fell through the roof of a barbed wire storage facility and as she lay dying on the piles of twisted metal, Bruno Santiago was born. The cuts inflicted upon the youngster were severe enough to scar him for life. The extra fingers? They once belonged to his mother.

Whatever story you believe doesn't detract from the fact that Bruno Santiago was a dirty old bastard, and only did his illegal transactions in one of two ways. *If you're a man, you pay in cash. If you're a woman, you suck my dick.*

Twenty minutes after arriving at Santiago's shack, Domino was leaving with a gun in her pocket, bullets in her hand and a disgusting taste in her mouth. Next stop, home.

Domino pushed open the door and could hear voices coming from the kitchen.
She paused to count the number of voices she could hear. Three, maybe four? As long as she shot straight, she had enough ammunition to go round.
Bang, BANG!

That afternoon Domino stood tall in the family kitchen. She was surrounded by empty beer bottles, smashed plates and four dead men. Her brothers and some random guy who was wearing a hat.
He doesn't have the hat now because Domino took it. She wears it as a trophy, a reminder of what had been.

As I write this, she has left her home and is travelling north, into the heart of Texas.
What happened next, I don't know.

King of the Trolls

Darnell Wash was a massive prick, and he knew it. He was *la troll extraordinaire* and he knew how to push the buttons of the online community. In the past 12 months he has had 4 Farcebook, 6 Instantgrim and 19 Twatter accounts banned / blocked / deleted, and this is why he exists. To shower people with abuse to the point where said social media channels decide to wave the wand of authority and remove him from their platform.

On Twatter he has gone by the following names;

Greg_hem0oroide_pop
TinaTurnips00o0
Fatnigel_hoohoo
Wa$$$hingtonFalles
AlanTrump3738227
pmurTdlanoDSQUEEZE
BiLiM911_119iMLiB
6839827649148275
Tony856986489638
Popped_Tart_Anal
Ice_Flaker_nnn
huhakjakvkaavavfilgh
GretalThumbticktack
Fake_News_Undrscor5e
TrollRoll_GashFlavourt
TrollRoll_MashFlavourt
QE2mingeBLACKSLASH
BingPingWingTing23582

Francis_dustalbin95

All of them troll accounts, all of them banned.

On Farcebook and Instantgram he followed the same pattern.
But why is he considered one of the nastiest people in recent (Western) history.
The reason being, he used what are now known as **'HURTY WORDS'**.
He shared an opinion that was not acceptable with the online community and because his opinion was different, he was labelled a racist, fascist and a Nazi. Generic insults were never going to make him change his opinion and in fact, made things worse.

Once upon a time there were three goats, and they were called Gruff. All three of them lived happily on a green hill, munching away at the fresh grass that was available. However, the grass soon ran out, because they were greedy.
This got them worried, and little billy goat gruff said, "What should we do now?" The biggest billy goat gruff said, "Let's go to the hill on the other end of the bridge. The grass is emerald green over there"

The goats decided to walk across the bridge to where the grass was emerald green, but unknown to them, a big troll lived under the bridge. The troll did not like those who were different to him and made a point of displaying his primitive insecurities onto anyone who dared to step onto the bridge.

*Little billy goat trotted along over the bridge. The troll he jumped up and yelled, "**Get the fuck off my bridge**," and in a matter of seconds ripped the smallest of the goats to shreds. His internal organs helped decorate the bridge in an unexpected red tone, and what remained was little more than a snack.*

After the brutal attack the other two goats decided it was probably best to avoid the bridge and stay where they were. With one less mouth to feed they felt that they would probably do ok, and that's that. The moral of the story? Beware of trolls. They're assholes and don't care who they hurt.

Darnell was that troll. Attacking the most vulnerable and the most reactive.
Pronouns were mocked. Attacks on the trans community were not only easy but also done with alarming regularity.
His favourite were those who are known as clout chasers. Desperate for a social media dopamine hit that would guarantee their digital standing and to be trending for at least the next couple of hours.

It's difficult to get one of these blue check mark liberals to engage with a regular person (or scum as they are sometimes referred to) but now and then he will trigger someone and it will get the reaction he is after and then the real shit starts to flow.
As soon as the digital trolls catch a wiff of some-

one falling they attack. Our man Darnell will then change to one of his many other aliases.

Darnell is dead now. Why? Because he went one step too far.
He trolled a young man by the name of Whiskey_Pyjamal, who was a young gay man and tweeted about a recent encounter he had with a local police officer. The post was littered with good humour, euphemisms and cheeky banter but Darnell took offense to this and moved in for the digital kill.

The posts author Whiskey_P was the type of guy who never took life seriously and would always bring humour and joy to any occasion. His post about the local 'Bobby on the beat' was a reflection of this. It was funny and made a lot of people laugh.
Darnell stood out from the crowd with his homophobic and aggressive replies, but this didn't bother Whiskey_P as he had dealt with many people like Darnell before. The way to deal with such ignorance and abuse is easy. Report. Block. And that is what he did.

This pissed Darnell off to the point that he threw his laptop against the wall and stormed out of the house.
He stomped off down the road and into the City Centre. Once there he entered the nearest pub and ordered a double vodka and coke. And then an-

other, and another.
Within two hours he was drunk. So drunk that the pub owner threw him out.
As Darnell stumbled around outside the pub, he couldn't quite work out which way he was supposed to go, so he decided that straight ahead was the best option.

As he walked forward and straight out into the road, he was run over by a bus and died immediately. Rubbish. What is the point. Really. Fuck everything. You're going to die anyway.

The end.

Frank Hunt. The Baby Sniper

During the winter of 1999, former army sniper Frank Hunt believed he was on a mission from God when he shot his first civilian. The victim survived but the baby she was carrying did not. Mary Macnamara was 33 weeks pregnant with her second child.

Twelve days later Frank struck again. Firing off 3 shots, killing 2 people and injuring another. Aisha Shafik was one of those shot and killed that day. She was 24 weeks pregnant.

Twenty days later Casey Blackman was gunned down. Shot multiple times and was 31 weeks pregnant.

Six days after, Lexi Hill was shot in the stomach. She survived but the baby she was carrying did not.

Three days later, he shot and killed Daisy Armstrong who was 27 weeks pregnant.

Nine days later, Franks body was dragged out of the Thames.

At the time there was nothing tying Frank to these shootings. The early conclusions were that Frank was just *another* white middle-aged man who couldn't face living any longer so decided to take his own life.

"Why do they have to make it so public?" asked DI Langstone.

"Make what so public?" asked Cream Tea.

"Suicide. It should be done in the privacy of your own home. Not out on display. Dragging other people into your dramatic sadness is the final act of a pathetic life that was no doubt full of bad decisions and ends with you standing on the edge of something, staring blankly into the distance as you mentally say goodbye to the world. A world, if truth be told, that doesn't give a monkeys bollock if you splat, bounce or walk away."

"A bit harsh isn't it boss?"

Langstone grinned at his junior *"Where's my coffee?"*

As Langstone sat waiting for his mid-morning refreshment he picked up the report on Frank Hunt. Without saying a word, Langstone got up and walked out of the office.

"Here's your coffee sir..." Cream Tea sighed and placed the cup next to the other cups that were full of unwanted coffee.

When Franks body was examined, he was found to be wearing something highly unusual, and can only really be described as an **artificial silicone pregnant belly bodysuit**. Not the whole body, just the belly area. The rest of the body belonged to Frank. The 6-foot, hairy, heavy build, Frank. On the surface of the silicone belly there what appeared to be pen marks. A five-bar tally gate and two other separate lines, about an inch in length. Seven, it totalled seven. But seven what?

Fast forward 18 days and Frank was confirmed to be the person behind the murders of 4 people and seriously injuring 3 others.
The 7 tally marks scribbled onto his silicone belly, could they be the 7 lives he attempted to take?
Of those who survived, there was one male, and he was shot in the leg so Frank would have known that this wouldn't have killed him. Frank was a well-seasoned professional, so clearly took that shot on purpose.
The focus of Franks attacks were on pregnant women, but that only accounts for 3 fatalities.
Maybe he wasn't trying to kill the mothers, but the babies?
Foetal deaths from these attacks still only add up to 5, so were there 2 that haven't been found yet?
Databases searched, phone calls made and still nothing.

Franks last known address; a ground floor studio flat in Croydon revealed nothing. Literally nothing. When Police entered the property, it was empty, apart from 3 items left of the laminate floor in the bathroom. A silver toaster, a broken Etch-a-sketch toy, and a framed photo of a heavily pregnant teenager. On the back of the photo were written these words.
'Half-sister. Bonded by blood, by envy.'

Even to this day police have been unable to identify the young woman in the photo or been able to determine what happened to her.

Herbie Rides, Again

"What, say that again."

"Someone tried to grow parsley in her."

Peacock didn't know what was going on, "I'm sorry Olly, can you say that again."

"Someone, tried to grow parsley in her."

Chris Peacock had been in the force for 19 years now but had never once heard anyone speak that sentence.

"What do you mean someone tried to grow parsley in her?"

Olly repeated, "Whoever killed her planted parsley seeds in cuts that were made in her skin, after she had died."

"So, what you're saying is, she was killed, sliced and then turned into a herb garden?"

Olly shrugged his shoulders, "Yeah I guess so."

Peacock walked past his colleague, "I want to see the body."

"She's downstairs with Sven." As Peacock swung the door open and left, Olly walked over to the office window and opened it wide. Twelve floors up not only provided Olly with a great view, but also with a great opportunity to end his life. Eight seconds later Olly's body splatted onto the street below.

Back inside the building, Peacock was entering the room and locked eyes with the onsite pathologist who simply shrugged his shoulders.

"How did she die," Peacock asked.

"It would appear she was force-fed stones until she could no longer breathe and died from suffocation."

"Force-fed stones?"

"Yes, as you can see…" the pathologist opened up the victims throat, "there are a number of different stones stuck within the oesophagus which has caused a great deal of damage to the oesophageal tissue but would have also led to a very slow and painful…"

"Shut up. Can you just tell me what happened in the simplest of terms. Pretend I'm stupid and explain it to me."

"Pretend? Ok, well the victim was most probably strapped to a chair or something where she remained in an upright position and these pebbles, stones, were forced down her throat until she stopped breathing. The killer then laid her out flat and cut her from the belly button up to…" Peacock interrupted again. "Up to her tits?"

"Yes. He then proceeded to very crudely sew the victim up and leave her naked body exposed in a garden which I can only assume was the victims garden"

Peacock walked away from the body and sat down. "Why did he sew the body up after he cut into her?"

"That I don't know yet. The seeds were found in separate cuts across her arms and thighs."

Peacock had a quick sniff of his fingers, grabbed a pen and started doodling.

"Excuse me sir, sorry but that's my report you're drawing on."

Peacock stopped as the paper was taken away from him. "Let me tell you something Doctor Sven. I am the senior officer here and if I want to draw on something, I will draw on it."
With that Peacock stood up and left the room.

"Doctor Sven? My name is Oliver Thomsen. Why do you not have any respect for anyone?"
Oliver threw his report to the floor and jumped out of the nearest window.

Five seconds later Olly's body landed with a thud on top of the other body.

Wednesday. Eighteen days after the *Parsley* body was found, another grim discovery was made.

This time it was the body of an elderly man. He was found in his garden where he was stripped naked and had stones forced into every available open space his body had to offer. Even his eyes were removed and the empty holes filled with stones.

His legs were cut open and investigations found that coriander seeds were planted into the open wounds.

Peacock led the investigation on this but once again revealed nothing.

Sixteen days later a third body was found and once again it was filled with stones and was massacred in much the same way as the others, except this time, the victims bum cheeks were sliced open and fennel seeds planted there.

Another death, another missed opportunity for Peacock to show his worth.

He was called to the office of his superior (Sir Oliver Greenwood) where he knew he was going to be challenged on the lack of progress he had made in regarding these three cases.

As Peacock entered the office, he found Sir Greenwood standing still with one foot on a chair and the other on the windowsill.

"Be a good chap," he said, "Pass me that yellow cloth on my desk would you."

Peacock moved forwards, reached over, and passed the old man the cloth.

"Thanks old chap. Must dash. Toodle bye."
With that he jumped out of the window and came to a sudden halt on the concrete below.

At his funeral, everyone spoke about what a great man he was and the stunning changes he made during his time in the force. He was certainly well loved and respected.

Peacock stood at the graveside as these final words were muttered by Sir Greenwoods only son.

"My dad was a unique and strong-willed individual who worked tirelessly to create a safer world for us all. His death was unexpected and serves as a reminder to all of us, just how quickly our lives can end."

The usual drinks session followed as everyone spoke about the greatness of Sir Greenwood.

On the walk home Peacock took a moment to reflect on the past few months. The bizarre human herb gardens he had been assigned to investigate and the unexpected deaths of his work colleagues. Maybe this had all become too much. He missed his own life. Maybe it was time to move on? Living so close to death, day after day, was beginning to take its toll and Peacock knew he had to take some time out, but how could he when he was still playing catch up. Still no closer to knowing the identity of 'Herbie'.

Three days later, Peacock was sat in his office drawing pictures of inverted lemons and limes when there was a knock at the door.

Peacock didn't answer because he knew it would be a new recruit. A new partner, associate, colleague or whatever you want to call them. The door knocked again and yet again it was ignored.

"Um, hello. I can see you. Can I come in and introduce myself."

"Yep." was the quick, blunt reply.

The door opened and a young, well presented man walked in. Dressed in a light blue suit with lilac shirt, he looked the part but was he going to be any good when it came to helping Peacock crack this *Herbie* case.

"What's your name lad."

"Wilkinson. Olly Wilkinson."

Peacock sighed as he stood up and opened the window, "Fuck sake. Here you are. See ya."

Olly smiled as he walked over to the open window and without hesitation, jumped out.

"What's the point," Peacock said to himself. "What's the fucking point."

Looking out of the window he saw the motionless body of another Olly and decided the best thing to do was to join him.

Peacock jumped the same way Olly did but as we know, when you jump in a dream you wake up! And that's exactly what happened here.

Olly woke up.

"You ok?" asked Charlotte.

"What, um yeah," Olly responded. "You know those dreams when you're falling and you wake up.."

Charlotte had fallen back to sleep.

"Fuck sake" muttered Olly and proceeded to pull back the duvet, climb out of bed, open the window and yes, you've guessed it. He jumped out.

Somehow there was already a body on the ground that managed to break his fall. Olly suffered a broken arm and a broken collarbone. The body he landed on was that of an old, retired police officer by the name of Chris Peacock.

Am I Dead?

"Where am I?"

"Don't you mean, when am I?"

"That doesn't make any sense."

"It does from where I'm standing."

"Oh, this is just a dream and you're being all weird because you're in my head."

"No I'm not."

"Yes you are. What do they call you? People that pop up in dreams, what you called?"

"I don't know, it's your dream."

"So you agree then that this is just a dream. My dream."

"No I don't, but you seem certain that you know what is going on."

"I am. I'm going to walk away from this now and find something else to dream about."

"Can you do that then?"

"Yeah, I have a whole world plotted out in my head. It's my safe space. Every part of it has been built by me and it's only when the big black train appears that I know there will be trouble."

"Big black train?"

"Yeah, it signals the beginning of an alien invasion and then I lose control of my dream and a battle begins."

"Sounds more like a nightmare."

"I like nightmares."

◆ ◆ ◆

"Why are you just standing there, smiling like a simpleton? I told you to leave."

"What do you want me to do?"

"Fuck off out of here. How many more times. This is my dream."

"Then remove me."

"I can't. Where is everything? There is no colour or depth to anything."

"What question do you want me to answer?"

"Where am I?"

"No, you mean.."

"Fuck off ok. Where am I if I'm not in own head."

"You are nowhere and somewhere. You are the past, present and future all rolled into one."

"What, the actual fuck are you talking about?"

"You are dead."

"What. Say that again."

"You are dead."

"What?"

"Listen, before you start with the questions and the angriness, let me give you some information in the most basic form possible. You died in your sleep from a massive heart attack. It was quick and you did not suffer any pain."

"Didn't suffer any pain. Whoopidy, fucking doo. What happens now?"

"Now? Nothing. Not until you've received all the information you need and then I will allow you to take the next part of your journey."

"Ok, what else do I need to know."

"When you died…"

"Whoa hang on a bastard minute. Why am I naked? Where are my clothes?"

"Why do you need clothes?"

"So you don't see my cock and balls of course. You're ok, you're wearing a dress I think?"

"Please, refrain from verbally attacking me and

interrupting me and all of this will become clear."

"Am I in Heaven or hell?"

"Please. Let me complete this induction."

"Induction! What the fuck."

"Please. Last warning or I will walk away, and you will just be left here, with nothing."

"I already have nothing."

"No, you have everything."

"Ok, I'll listen."

"You died on the 20th day of March, 2003. Jump forward 173 years, 3 months and 4 days and you will find yourself here today, which is Monday, March 24, 2176."

"I've been dead for 170 years."

"You died on Earth 173 years ago and yesterday your name was said for the final time. Never again will anyone on Earth say your name."

"What about my family. My, my family?"

"All passed. Those that remain do not know you and will never know you."

"I feel sick."

"This will pass, although it is not sickness you feel but the feeling of emptiness. The realisation that everyone and everything you had ever loved has gone. The realisation that you are alone. The false sense of dread and fear that will wash over you like a wave of fire, but it will pass."

"Can you give me a moment to just understand what is going on right now. Yesterday I had a shit day at work, sunk a few beers and was in bed by 11, and now 170 years later I've woken up, dead, naked and talking to a guy that says I have everything. I have nothing. Do you understand NOTHING."

"I will give you a moment to process what has just happened."

"Let me ask one question and I want a straight answer. Why did it take 170 whatever it is, years for me to be woken up?"

"173 years. The reason is that when humans pass to this moment, they bring with them emotional baggage in the shape of concerns and questions about their loved ones. It's understandable, but it is also an unwanted distraction. We have found over time that this process works best as, in your case, no one on Earth will speak your name again. You are gone, lost, forgotten. It is now time for you to move onto the next phase of your journey."

"Next phase? Wait. I don't like the answer you just gave me. What do you mean an unwanted distraction. This is my family I'm talking about. I want to see them. Make sure they are alright."

"And therein lies is the problem. You can't because they are not here. When their time is up they will go through the same process as you."

"So, what if you die young?"

"Then you will be delivered here much quicker as it is probable that people will stop talking about you a lot quicker as you made less impact on the world."

"What about Kings and Queens? Key figures in history. They always get spoken about."

"And as a result, they will never move on. Glory in one life does not transfer to the next."

"So, as long as people continue to talk about Adolf Hitler, he will never move onto this bit. Is that right?"

"Yes."

"I get that as a punishment but what about great people. Tolstoy for example. He will always be a point of conversation so again he will never get here."

"Correct. Like Hitler, Tolstoy will remain in limbo until the time comes when he is no longer mentioned."

"Will that day ever come?"

"Of course. That day will come for all of us."

"I have so many questions…"

"I'm sure you do but now is not the time."

"Why not? I'm not going anywhere. I mean, I have all the time in the world now. Don't I?"

"Time does not exist where we are."

"Yes it does. You told me I died 173 years ago."

"That is in Earth years. Human years. I have to offer you a timescale to which you would understand. Years, months and days, much like hours and minutes are timescales you know about but here, now, time does not exist."

"But we've been talking. That has taken time."

"No, it hasn't."

"This is annoying me now. If this is a dream, I want it to end. NOW."

◆ ◆ ◆

"Nothing. Typical, nothing. So this is my life now is it."

"This is the next stage of your journey. You had life on Earth, that has ended and…"

"What about Mummies? No one spoke about them for years so they must have come back but then had to go again when their bodies were found."

"No, they never arrived. We knew their names would be spoken again so they remained in their graves."

"What would happen if the world blew up? Mankind was wiped out? Hang on, what do you mean you knew their names would be spoken again? You know when it's time for someone to arrive here? Has my wife arrived? Is she here?"

"The term wife does not exist. The love between two people does not exist."

"What about soulmates?"

"It's just a phrase. Do you believe that those who once dwelled in caves had soulmates? I won't insult you by making you answer that because the answer is, no."

"And the exploding world?"

"If mankind was to be wiped from Earth, then they would all arrive at once and we would move on to the next part of the journey."

"What is this journey you keep harping on about?"

"Are you ready?"

"I don't know because I don't know what it is."

"So, I will wait."

"How long will that take? No, don't answer that I already know what you're going to say."

"So, I will wait."

"If time doesn't exist, how can you wait?"

"I use words and terminology that you will understand. You understand the context in which the word *wait* can be used so that is why I used it."

"Fuck sake. Look I am tired of this. Please let me move on or die. If I'm dead, let me die."

"Is that what you want, to be gone. To be nothing?"

"I am nothing. How can I be anything other than nothing. I have nothing."

"You have every..."

"Don't. Just don't. I stand here before you, butt naked and not knowing what is going on. All you've done is be cryptic and given me no real answers to my questions. At least answer one question, please!"

"Ok, ask me."

"Where am I?"

"Here."

"Oh, you are a prick. Kill me yeah. End me. Whatever it is you're actually capable of doing."

"Are you sure?"

"Yes, I've had enough of this. Make me dead again."

Catch Me If You Want

"Hello I'm here to see Burton Wallace."
"Of course, and who are you?"
"I'm a friend of his grandson."
"Is Mr Wallace expecting you?"
"No, I have something I need to ask him. I know Carl looks up to his grandfather and would want this done the right way."
"Ooh, sounds interesting."
"I'm going to ask for his permission as me and Carl wish to marry."
"Congratulations!"
"Well, he hasn't agreed yet. I'll let you know on my way out what he says."
"Exciting. Yes, let me know how you get on
"Thank you, will do. Am I ok to go through?"

"Yes of course. Good luck."

Burton Wallace was to become the third victim in as many days as Lewis made his way from random care home to random care home in an attempt to end the lives of as many as he could before he got caught.
He knew he'd get caught, but the game was to see how many he could chalk up before that day happened.

As mentioned, Burton was number three, and Hazel Graham would be the last victim at number six.

Six kills in six days.
Six bizarre selfies which were posted online and have since been removed.
Six elderly people that were happy to have a visitor but were never going to welcome another visitor again.

With every visit he carried with him a mask. It wasn't a decent mask, but it did its job.
On day one he posed with Roberta Englund whist wearing a cheap horror film mask.
He had already inserted three knives into her head and the fourth one was in his hand, implying it was soon to be inserted into her left eye. After the selfie was taken, it was.

He posted his kills up onto social media but for the first few days no one cared. That wasn't a concern as he knew someone would pick up on this at some point, and they did.

Lewis began in Edgbaston and his final kill was in Dudley.

In that time, he wore six different masks but killed the old folks in pretty much the same way. Knives inserted into their heads and, well, that's it really.
Police reports suggest that the attacks were extremely violent but quick. The victims wouldn't have had much time to get a grasp of what was going on before the first knife was inserted. It has been suggested that the victims were dead within

seconds, so the suffering was brief.

On the sixth day Lewis visited Hazel. Posed once again as a family member and was allowed access to her room without supervision.

On entering the room, Hazel didn't recognise who this young man was. That didn't stop her from being victim six.
One knife inserted into the left eye, another in the right temple and a third knife in the throat. Lewis was once again wearing a mask, this time it was a hockey mask, reminiscent of the one worn by Jason Voorhees. Except this time the mask was a cheap replica and looked every bit it's £2.50 worth.

Lewis took a selfie and uploaded it to social media. As he did so the door burst opened and in walked Ramboo.
"I told you, I'll be back." he boomed.
Releasing the safety off his gun, he took aim and blasted Lewis until he resembled nothing more than a human trifle.

Outside, the crowds gathered as Ramboo walked down the great hall to collect his medal. Triumphant flute music could be heard floating over the hills, as Julie Andrews picked posies with drunken children. Geese flew overhead dropping various baseball mascots onto the heads of the cheering crowd.
As Ramboo got nearer to the stage, he noticed a small otter sobbing.

"What's wrong little otter." he mumbled.
"It's the charabanc sir. It has no wheels."

A - Z
We learn this first, then G-O-D follows

Alice Malice was the name of his wife
He sliced her open with his knife
She cried and whimpered for her life
But Zachary skipped away

Bobby Stocks had seen all this
He tried to help but instead he missed
A flying blade, a final kiss
As Zachary skipped away

Craig Potato had a stammer
He tried to cure it with a hammer
This killing game is not all glamour
Is what Zachary used to say

His true first love was **D**ani Duck
Who loved to sing and loved to fuck
But then one day she was out of luck
As Zachary skipped away

Eddie Richard gave us hope
Acting the fool, acting the dope
Did it last, the answer nope
As Zachary skipped away

Fish and chips were best for tea
Batter thick and full of grease
Meat and oil, shit and pee
Infected from a young age

GET OUT was the first recorded
A song at college now aborted
The bass was clean but now distorted
Young Zachary does not play

Harry Diamond was a cunt
What word is there that rhymes with cunt
Blah, blah, blah, blah, blah, blah cunt
And Zachary made him pay

Internal fury, external blood
Soiled forever this puddle of mud
We fell to earth with a mighty thud
As Zachary came to play

Jump to death and die in glory
You splat creating something gory
Tomorrow sadness, tomorrow story
Shadows do not lay

Kelly ran and joined them hoping
They would stop their heavy groping
The kid that led the hands was scoping
Ways to make her stay

The **L**aw was half of his birth name
He fought the Law and won that game
But all the losers look the same
When Zachary wants to play

Maxi Disco was just a man
Built with a penis and a plan
He changed his name to Sexy Jan

When Zachary chose to pay

Now do not think that is done
We've only just started the fun
Needle, blade or easy gun
Decisions, to be made

Oh
Please
Quit
Replaying
Stupid
Tedious
Unimpressive
Videos
When
Xavier
Yells
Zachary has walked away

Have you ever played the Alphabet Game? How you play is as follows.

Pick a category, so let's say for example the category is films, and for the purpose of this example there are 3 people playing.

Person 1 goes first with A. Name a film that starts with the letter A. **Alien**.

Person 2 has B and may answer **Bad Boys**.

Person 3 has C and may answer **Catch Me If You Can**.

It then goes back to person 1 who has D. Person 2 has E, and so on.

The other way of playing is to have all 3 people answer the same letter.

Person 1 with the letter A would possibly say **Alien**.

Person 2 could say **Air Force One**, and person 3 might say **A Nightmare on Elm Street**.

Letter B begins with person 3 who might say **Bambi**. Person 2 says **Batman Begins** and person 1 goes with **Babe**.

Letter C then begins again with person A, followed by 2 then 3. It then goes back from 3, 2 to 1.

Alphabet games are a great way to kill time if your sat waiting for a bus or waiting for a coffin to burn during a cremation. It's light-hearted entertainment, but what if it became a matter of life and death. The alphabet became not just the game, but also the solution. A game of cat and mouse as someone is hunted across the country. You could begin in Aberdeen then move onto Bath, then Cardiff. Or, make it more contained within the borders of England.

Aldershot, **B**ristol, **C**ambridge, **D**erby, **E**xeter, **F**areham, **G**illingham, **H**ull, **I**pswich... overshot myself with **J**.

But, it would be very cool to produce a piece of work that was 26 chapters long.

I could call it; *A to Z, a matter of Life and Death*, or, the *Really, Really Serious Alphabet Game*.

26 ways to kill someone?

26 places to visit and kill?

2+6=8

Using a basic A1Z26 decoding cipher, or whatever it's called, the word GOD = 8

7+15+4= 26
2+6= 8

I would become GOD.

I would be playing GOD with their lives and once the 26 is complete, I will be complete.
I will finally become the man you wanted me to be. Abusive, full of hatred and anger, but still a GOD.

You would stand at my piss stained alter and prey as I snap off your fingers, one at a time.
Without fingers you could no longer prey in a way that I would consider appropriate and as a result I will send you and your stumpy hands straight to Hell.
Your severed fingers would be added to my collection and when my mission is complete, I will have accumulated 260 fingers and thumbs. A fine collection of digits. Once I have returned to my shelter I will procced in building a model church from the pieces I have collected and once constructed, I shall paint it black and leave it outside the doors of some big old, pretentious art gallery.
Within a few days it will be showcased, and people will come from far and wide to look at this bizarre piece of Outsider Art. But then, during **National**

Allow Dogs into Galleries Day which I believe is in June, a young bitch will get a wiff of mouldy fingers and knock the church from its mantle. A few minutes later the floor will be covered with a variety of different sizes, colours and textures of human fingers. It will be then that the true horror of what has been standing proudly within the Gallery was nothing more than a homage to murder, or a shrine to GOD. As with all art, it's open to interpretation.

RAIN

It's raining again. To be honest it's been raining every day for the past couple of weeks. Even when the skies are blue and the sun in beaming, it's raining.

I've managed to stay dry as I haven't been outside since the rain started but I think I will have to go outside soon as I'm starting to get hungry.

The cupboard is almost empty, the fridge is turned off and the milk smells like, well, let's just say the milk smells, and to be fair is probably thicker than it should be.

Maybe I could make cheese? Cottage cheese! But I don't know how to make cottage cheese. Maybe I'll just leave the milk and see what happens.

My friend came over again yesterday. I didn't answer the door, but she shouted through the letterbox that she is going to speak to my mum because I need help. I don't need help, I need shopping. My mum won't come over I know that because we don't really get on. Never have. I think she blames me for ruining her vag or something? I don't know and I don't care. Honestly don't care. The last time we spoke we argued. A stupid argument about the milk.

I miss my mum. A real mum. I mean, I miss something I never had. I just want someone I can turn to when I need to. A mother that cares. A mother that looks at me the same way, every day. With love and compassion not CONpassion.

My mum is a fraud. A parent by name only. When it rains, she is not there to help me or offer shelter. She just cheers on the clouds and hopes the rain continues for another day because she knows I can't speak to her when it rains. I can't speak to anyone.

My mouth fills with water and I'm drowning. The rain keeps pouring into my lungs and I cannot breathe.

I look up and see nothing but black clouds as the rain keeps pouring.

She, the mother, stands and watches and waits until I'm gone.

I'll be gone soon enough, then she can leave and forget I ever existed.

Maybe then the sun will come out.

WHOLE TRUTH?

Hello, my name is Keith. I'm a 28-year-old female from Warrington and a compulsive liar. I am vegetarian but that's not important. I'm also a devout Christian but again that's not important.

What is important is that I'm able to talk to you and you are listening. We are conversing. Okay, it's a one-way conversation but you're here, I'm here so let's do this.

Who am I?

Maybe I'm a 41-year-old male from Scarborough

with cancer.
Maybe I'm a 14-year-old who has been abused by her stepfather.
Maybe I am the stepfather.
Maybe I'm the guy who listened to his sisters' story and hunted down the bastard who abused her and killed him.
Maybe I'm just a geography teacher from Cardiff.

Text is deceptive. I could be anyone yet what I write you will take for granted. You will take as fact because it's written down.

A diagnosis, a test result, a story, a confession.
A reason to believe something or someone.
A text, an email or a candid Facebook message from a well-being stranger telling you that the love of your life has been fucking your brother.
Yes, your boyfriend is gay!
But is he?
What do you want to believe?

My name is Keith and I'm a 38-year-old male from Warrington and I am a compulsive liar.
My favourite meal is a bacon burger with cheese and extra bacon. I am agnostic. I am a compulsive liar. Why, because my fantasy is more acceptable than your reality. I hate the world you have created and the sheds of shit you call a home. I have struggled my whole life to fit in and be a productive member of society yet all that happens is, I get beaten down.

Beaten down to nothing. This led me to create my own existence. One that is better than yours because I control it. I know who I can trust, and I know who I can tell the truth to. Problem is, I no longer know what the truth is.

All I know is that one day I will be dead, and you won't care. Telling the truth or not, really it doesn't matter.

When

When I cut, I drip dust
An uncomfortable experience
But one I must complete at least once a week
If I don't, then the dust builds, and I can't breathe
Blades of steel are hidden away
In secret places
Ready and waiting
Expecting to go to work
They smile when I touch them

When I cut, I drip dust
I punch clouds of vapour, but nothing moves
No dents, no impact
Yet still I punch, over and over
When I cry my eyes stay dry
Inside I'm wet but there's a disconnect
Tears won't fall no matter how hard I try
Pass me a tissue, pretend that you care

This isn't a story
Not one you can relate to

I may try and reach out, but it is nothing more than attention seeking
My headstone will remind you that I felt that way
Push your tears back in, I don't need them
Save them for yourself, pity
Pathetic
People
You shall not be missed

The GoD

The Grand old duke of York
He's killed twenty four men
He led the pigs to the top of the hill
And led them down again

When I am up, I stay up
When they think that I'm down they stay down
But I hide away and fuck them up
Am I up or am I down?

Printed in Great Britain
by Amazon